Hunter's Captive

by

Cassandra Bella

Hunter's Captive

Cover Art by *RJ Morris*

The Wild Rose Press, Inc.
PO Box 708
Adams Basin, NY 14410-0708
Visit us at www.thewildrosepress.com

Publishing History
First Crimson Rose Edition, 2017
Print ISBN 978-1-5092-1312-2
Digital ISBN 978-1-5092-1313-9

Published in the United States of America

"Damn you." His harsh voice
broke through the eerie silence. "Damn you for making me still want you after you stole away everything there was between us."

His lips closed over hers, punishing her for what she had done. His hands fisted in her hair, holding her almost painfully to his kiss. He was trying to hurt her just as she had hurt him. His kiss, his hold, was not of tenderness and love. It sparked with anger and frustration.

Bruising her soft lips, he forced her mouth to open. She knew she should break away, but she couldn't do it. Instead, she met his kiss with the same fierce response as desperation and need swelled around her.

He groaned low and hard, his hands releasing their hold on her hair, skimming down her body. They circled around her slender waist. Pulling her flush against him, he rubbed her against the bulge threatening to break through his jeans. His fingers pushed into her skin, holding her where he wanted her.

Dedication

In memory of
my wonderful uncle, Joseph Kim Bella.
One Christmas morning long ago,
you gave me a journal and said,
"The best thing a writer can do is write."
I still have that journal,
and the memory of your words, to this day.
You always believed in me!

Prologue

He'd forgotten how brilliantly the Colorado sun could shine on a warm summer day.

Hunter Reese stared out the small, cubbyhole window, catching a glimpse of the Denver skyline as the day pulled to a close. From the tenth floor, he had a bird's-eye view of anxious workers scampering along the streets of lower downtown, finding their way home.

His dark mustache jumping as he spoke, Special Agent in Charge, Marcus Williams continued his run down for the following day. His steely gaze demanded attention as he took in the handful of agents around him, lingering on Hunter before moving on.

With a slight shift of his elbow, Wallace Smith poked his partner in the ribs, pulling Hunter's attention away from the window. He knew he wasn't missing a word, but Williams had the look. The one every agent understood and knew not to ignore.

Hunter forced away the troubling thoughts clouding his mind. He knew this would happen the minute he received the call ordering him and Smith on the first flight to Denver. Had it not been for an emergency with another agent assigned to the case, he'd still be in Washington, far away from the troubling memories.

Yet here he was, inside this hot, closed-in room, wishing he'd been called to anywhere else in the world.

Here, was his hometown. Here, was the place he'd done his best to avoid for the past ten years. And he'd been successful at it, until now.

"We've got confirmation on Grant Robinson's whereabouts tomorrow afternoon," Williams continued. "Our suspect is to be married at exactly two o'clock."

Digging into his briefcase, he pulled out a plain manila envelope. "His bride-to-be is a well-known socialite around these parts. Their wedding has been talked about for months. Everyone who is anyone is expected to attend and I wouldn't be surprised if we have some high-ranking officials on the guest list as well as Denver's elite."

Hunter's mouth tightened into a scowl at the mention of Denver's upper class. He knew, all too well, the money and prestige residing in this town. Though there was true greatness in some, others chose to follow their own rules, careful not to mix with the lower side of the city. With those like him who'd experienced, first hand, the darker side of such a diverse city.

"This is Grant's wife-to-be." Williams tossed a picture onto the table. Hunter ignored it. They all looked the same to him. "We have no evidence she's involved. But the Bureau wants to take her in for questioning just the same."

Beside him, Smith picked up the photo, giving it a once over. "Do we have a name on her?" He tossed it back to the center of the table.

Williams nodded. "Paxton Walsh."

Hunter's blood turned to ice. His heart stopped in mid-beat, the name echoing inside his head. He couldn't have heard right. "What was the name again?" He kept his tone flat, uninterested.

"Paxton Walsh," Williams repeated. "Her family goes back through the generations in this area. Her great-grandmother was responsible for bringing much of the culture into the city. And her grandfather spent years entwined in Denver's political best, earning a long running respect for her family name."

Paxton Walsh. A cold shiver raced up his spine. It was a name he'd avoided for ten years. One he'd tried hard to forget. The photo in the center of the table turned dark and ominous. He had to look at it, had to know, but his hands refused to move.

Every muscle in his body screamed in protest as he reached for the photo. Holding it in front of him, he prayed he wouldn't recognize the woman staring back at him. There was a slim chance there were two Paxton Walshes in the city.

Even as he fed himself the lies, he knew they were ridiculous. Only one person carried the wealth and prestige Williams described. Only one family in Denver's elite carried such a legacy.

A set of sapphire blue eyes stared back at him through a stream of long, thick lashes. Those eyes. He knew them all too well. They once haunted his dreams and taunted him with bitter memories he couldn't forget. Even through the flat effect of the photo, they reached out to him, grabbing at a part of his heart he kept well hidden.

He didn't need a longer look to confirm his worst nightmare. Somehow, some way, fate brought him back to this town, this life he'd left behind. And in a cruel twist, he found himself in the path of the one woman he'd hoped he would never see again.

"So what is the plan for tomorrow?" Smith's

question filtered through but barely registered.

Williams rubbed at the rough stubble lining his rounded jaw. "Seems to me, it would be a shame to upset such a highly anticipated event. There's sure to be enough high-ranking officials there to cause a stir if we make a big commotion before the nuptials."

"So we let them go ahead with the wedding?"

Hunter struggled to bring his attention back where it belonged. With an effort he'd used many times before, he shoved down old memories, burying them deep in his gut.

Williams nodded. "After the ceremony, our agents will wait outside to apprehend Robinson. If we're lucky, most of the guests will have made it to the reception by then and we'll avoid a large, ugly scene."

"What about Paxton Walsh?" Smith slid the picture from Hunter's sight and pushed it closer to William's reach.

"She'll be taken into custody, though I doubt there'll be reason to hold her." Williams collected the picture and tucked it back into the envelope. "We'll question her, see what we can get. But I don't think there's much she knows to help us."

"What about the informant?" True to his character, Smith pushed for more information. It was an annoying trait but made him one of the best agents in the Bureau. "Are we sure he'll testify? Without him, we don't have a case."

"He'll testify." There wasn't a trace of doubt in William's words. "He's looking for a lighter sentence. He knows testifying is the only way he'll get it."

"So it's a wrap then?" Smith pushed up from his seat.

Williams nodded, dismissing the group. "Reese, I need a minute before you go." He moved aside, allowing the others agents to file out of the small room.

Hunter waited in his seat while they cleared out. Once the last one disappeared, he stood, crossing the room to where Williams waited.

"Is there something you want to tell me?" He wasted no time with small talk.

Williams hadn't become a top-notch agent by chance. He was good. Good enough to notice when one of the agents under his command was distracted from the case before him. He knew something was up, but Hunter wasn't about to indulge him with information.

"It's nothing I can't handle," he assured his commanding officer. "Just a touch of the past. Nothing more."

"We can't have mistakes on this." Williams gathered the manila envelope into his hands, the sight of it reminding Hunter of the picture inside. "Our agents have worked too hard and too long. I'm not about to let it slip away when we finally have our first true break."

"There won't be any mistakes," Hunter promised, reaching for the door. "As I said, it's nothing."

Receiving the nod dismissing him, he stepped out of the room. He hadn't lied. Enough time had passed, enough lonely years without her. Being in the mix of Paxton all over again was something he'd handle just fine. He had a job to do. Nothing more, nothing less.

"So you've already worked up our SAC." Standing outside the door, Smith pushed away from the wall he'd hitched a shoulder to, falling into step beside his partner.

"Williams has a problem getting worked up over nothing," Hunter grumbled, heading for the elevator. Reaching it before the doors closed, he waited for Smith to join him then hit the button for the ground floor.

"Took some time figuring out what was going on in there. Wasn't till I was out of the room, giving it some thought, I realized what has you so tense."

Hunter glanced at his partner. How in the hell did Smith know anything about the past he'd left behind?

From deep in his memory came a vague recollection of a night spent inside a dark, smoky bar, downing one too many shots of Jack. His tongue loosened by alcohol, he shared more than he should have. How much, he couldn't be sure. But obviously it was more than he'd thought.

"The Paxton in that picture is the same one you told me about, isn't she?"

An awful throbbing began in Hunter's right temple. He should have known that night would come back to haunt him.

"She *is* the same," Smith determined from his partner's silence. He let out a low, knowing whistle. "Did you tell Williams?"

Hunter shook his head. "There's no reason for him to know anything. Paxton was a long time ago. My past with her has nothing to do with this case."

Smith's answering look was laced with doubt. "I hope you don't get yourself into a mess with this. The Bureau isn't going to be happy if something happens to put a damper on their case."

"Like I told, Williams, there's nothing to worry about." Irritation sliced heavy in Hunter's words. The day had definitely gone downhill. He should have turned down the case from the very beginning. Coming back to Denver was a stupid move.

Smith held up a large, rough hand in defense. "All right. This is your call. If you think you can handle it, I won't argue."

Hunter nodded, grateful the questions had stopped.

"So you feel up to grabbing a quick beer before heading back to the hotel?" Smith stepped out as the elevator doors slid open. Together, they cut a path through the potted plants, growing like a jungle inside the plush lobby.

"I think I'll pass." Hunter pushed on the heavy glass door leading outside. "It's been a long day and my bed is calling."

The sounds of cars whizzing by and people rushing along the sidewalk washed over them as they joined the constant clamor of downtown. A light evening breeze swirled, kicking the acrid scent of exhaust into the air.

Smith shrugged. "Well, I need that beer. I'll catch a cab back to the hotel."

With a wave, he headed off in the opposite direction. Hunter watched him disappear around the corner then turned for the parking garage. His dark blue rental car was right where he'd left it. Within minutes, he was behind the wheel, guiding the compact sedan down the busy streets.

****

Night had long ago fallen and yet Hunter continued his vigil, staring out the window of his tiny hotel room. During the day, he had a view of the Rocky Mountains, jetting high into the sky, peaks capped with snow. At night, the view changed, darkness blanketing the twinkling lights of the suburbs surrounding Denver.

Once the shock of Paxton being a part of his latest case subsided, other thoughts clouded his mind. The knowledge of what she was about to experience put a foul taste in his mouth.

Her memory might bring forth an old anger from deep inside but that didn't change his belief she wasn't a criminal. She couldn't know what Grant was up to. Williams pretty much said so himself.

After lying dormant for so long, old protective instincts kicked to life. His first irrational thought was to find a way to shield her from what was coming and protect her from the terror she'd face.

Naïve in most ways of the world, she wasn't going to hold up well. She'd be questioned by some of the best agents in the bureau. Agents who didn't believe in being easy with anyone. He saw a bewildered Paxton locked inside a tiny, stuffy room, frightened, and uncertain of what was happening.

Damn. He shoved away from the window and made a straight line for the wet bar on the other side of the room. Pouring a hefty helping of Scotch, he downed it in one large swallow then refilled his glass.

Amber liquid swirled, ice cracking against the sides of the glass as he paced. Large strides quickly ate up the space between each wall.

What did he care what happened to her? She was no longer a part of his life. Hadn't been for a long time. Whatever messes she fell into were her own doing. They didn't concern him.

She'd made it clear ten years ago how she felt about him being a part of her life. He'd followed her wishes, never again letting their paths cross. There wasn't any reason for him to step in now.

Whatever she had waiting down the road, she'd have to handle it alone. He only had to be kicked once in the gut to know when not to make the same mistake twice. And anything pertaining to Paxton Walsh was most definitely a mistake.

Chapter One

It was the perfect day for an even more perfect June wedding. The sun shimmered bright and brilliant in the early afternoon sky. From the treetops in City Park, the song of birds rose over the constant rush of traffic, blaring horns, and squeaking brakes.

A warm breeze settled in the air, clearing away the fog of pollution and leaving behind the sweet scent of freshly bloomed flowers tumbling from pots along the sidewalk.

To the average eye, nothing appeared out of the ordinary. Wedding guests stopped to chat in groups before making their way up the stairs toward the large, gray-stoned church. Limousines lined the street on both sides, drivers in crisp, pressed suits holding open the doors.

Women in elegant dresses, diamonds and gold glittering from their wrists and necks, walked at the sides of their well-tailored husbands. Prestige and wealth was evident with every turn of the head. The shine of money, new and old, hung like a halo over it all.

Standing across the street from the church, Hunter knew things weren't always as they seemed. Nondescript vehicles hugged curbs around the church as a low-keyed flutter of activity waved in the air. Some on the streets weren't invited guests, but holding true to their training, they blended with the others, calling no attention to themselves.

Overhead, the church bells chimed, signaling the guests to find their seats.

Slipping in with a passing group, he followed the flow up the rock-carved stairs, into the church's naturally cooler interior. He pushed away as the group continued into the chapel, finding a long, deep hallway cutting through the back.

Silence met him, an eerie contrast to the clamor he'd left behind. He had no idea what he was doing or what had brought him inside when his assigned position was along the perimeter.

He was going against orders, yet he couldn't bring himself to leave. Something held him back though he fought against the truth of it.

A light, airy laugh broke through the quiet, bringing him up short. He knew that laugh. Had heard it many times. Only one person had a laugh so soft and delicate it floated like a feather through the air. Only one was as beautiful in sound as she was in person.

A door off the side of the hallway creaked open, forcing him back into the shadows. A circle of pink chiffon floated from the room, and half a dozen women giggled their way toward the front of the church, taking no notice of the strange man they passed on their way.

Bride's maids.

And wherever there were bride's maids there was sure to be a bride. He inched down the hall to the open door. Careful not to make a sound, he curved around the frame, slipping inside.

Sunlight peeked through the windows, dancing delicate rays over the middle of a small reception area.

His steps silent along the polished wood floor, he pushed between two large, potted ferns and stood unseen behind matching loveseats filling the limited space.

He settled his attention toward the back of the room where a small dressing area had been cautiously constructed. Cosmetics lined one long table, brushes and compacts tossed about everywhere. A large mirror propped up against the far wall reflected his image, a silky slip hanging from the corner. Jeans, shirts, socks, and shoes, scattered the floor only a few inches away.

It was chaos. Yet none of it held his attention for long as he was drawn to something much more intriguing.

She stood to the side, a waterfall of white lace. Her back was to him, providing an uninterrupted chance to let his curious gaze travel over her. Honey-blond hair tumbled in layers over her shoulders. The gown, clinging to her slender body, sliced down her back, leaving a delectable swath of creamy white skin. She sighed, gently lifting her tiny shoulders, sending a wave of curls falling to the side.

He took a step, but the wooden floor chose to end its silence, creaking under his weight. The sound echoed through the room.

She turned, a soft smile caressing her full lips. Sapphire eyes locked with his, washing away the smile. A cold stare reached across the distance. For a breath in time, the world stopped spinning. The seconds stopped ticking away. Everything froze in that instant of recognition for the man standing before her.

****

Paxton struggled to regain the breath that rushed

from her lungs. Numb from head to toe, she grasped for some sort of stability to bring her back to reason.

Hunter Reese.

Where in the world had he come from?

She had to be dreaming. He was a mirage, an illusion having nothing to do with reality. After all these years, all this time, it was impossible to believe he stood before her, as handsome and rugged as ever.

"Hunter." She fought to stay on two feet with knees wobbling and weak.

He didn't say a word or move a muscle. He just stood there, staring at her, his deep gray eyes flickering over her, the heat from them burning her skin.

In only minutes, she was to marry Grant and before her stood the only man who had ever held the key to her heart. The one man she had ever truly loved.

This wasn't possible. She had to be dreaming. Hunter Reese was part of her past. He didn't belong here on her first step into a brand new future.

He took a step, and she fought the urge to back away. Inch by agonizing inch he came closer. He said nothing, his eerie silence sending a shiver up her spine. Stopping with only an inch between them, dark, clouded eyes bore straight through her. The warmth of his breath brushed against her cheek.

Seconds felt like hours as he stood there with his lips forming a tight, grim line. The creases in his forehead stretched fiercely over his brow.

What did he want? Why was he here?

Before she could ask, he took another step, his arms settling around her slender waist. In the flash of a second, giving her no chance to respond, he hoisted her off her feet. White lace bunched against his arms as he tossed her over his shoulder. He turned for the door; his hold tight as he nudged it open with his knee, carried her out of the room.

They were halfway down the hall before she regained some control. She closed her gaping mouth with a violent snap and kicked her legs. Twisting from side to side, she fought to break free.

"What in the world are you doing?" She couldn't see where they were going, only what they left behind. "If you don't put me down, I swear I'll start screaming at the top of my lungs."

Lowering her just enough to reach around with the arm that had been holding her steady, he clamped a firm hand over her mouth. She sputtered over the sudden barrier, unable to utter another word through the thickness of his palm.

The reality of what was happening settling in, she bared her teeth. Finding the tender skin between his thumb and index finger, she clamped down as hard as she could. Satisfaction soared as he cursed from the pain.

Still, he didn't let go.

This couldn't be happening. She kicked in a fury, the pointed toe of her satin shoe making contact with his leg. Any minute now someone was going to turn down the hallway and see what was happening. Any minute now they'd appear to stop whatever crazy scheme he had in mind.

Any minute now.

The hallway remained empty. Only minutes earlier it had been bustling with activity and now it lay motionless. Not a soul was in sight. The dressing room grew farther and farther away as Hunter's rushed steps took them deeper into the back of the church.

Desperation had a tight grip on her nerves. She opened her mouth, attempting to speak, but Hunter's hand still held tight. Her wiggling and kicking hadn't accomplished anything. She was helpless in the arms of a man she was convinced had lost his mind and gone way off the deep end.

Door hinges creaked a second before a blast of sunlight showered over her. Over Hunter's shoulder, she watched the heavy metal door swing shut. The dull thud left finality in its wake.

She struggled to get away. Somehow, someway, she had to break free. She didn't have any idea what he had in mind. He led her away from the back door, maneuvering them through the rows of cars crammed into the tiny parking lot behind the church.

The man was crazy. That was the only answer she could find explaining his actions. Over the past ten years, something inside must have cracked, leaving a mad man instead.

One she had to get away from.

Hunter stopped short at a royal blue Cherokee parked toward the back of the lot. "Nice plates." He shifted her weight over his shoulder, grabbing the handle of the driver's door.

She cursed the personalized plates she'd ordered. With her name splattered below the back fender, he had no problem finding what he was looking for. She knew what he would locate next and gritted her teeth against the frustration settling in.

Her body leaned forward with his as he opened the unlocked door and leaned inside the sun-burned interior. With a flick of his wrist, he pulled the visor down, bringing a set of keys tumbling into his grasp.

"I always told you it was asking for trouble having personalized plates and leaving your keys in the car." He shook his head. "Ten years and you're still so predictable."

Desperate, she watched the back door of the church, praying for somebody to find their way outside. She wasn't a fool. Hunter had a car and keys. He wasn't planning to stick around and was obviously set on taking her along with him.

She struggled in vain while he squeezed them through the driver's door. Dropping her onto the passenger seat, he pulled the door shut while hitting the automatic door locks. Even as she scrambled to unlock the car, he kept hold of the little lever, preventing her side from working.

"Damn you." She turned on him. "Let me out of here."

He didn't respond as he turned the engine over and brought the car to life with a gentle hum. His silence stroked the raging fire behind her anger. "You're crazy." She continued her relentless pursuit on the locks.

When she moved to the button to roll down the windows, she found, again, he'd beaten her to the punch. Engaging the lock mechanism on the side of his door, he prevented any of the windows from rolling down.

This was unbelievable. Ten years had slipped by without a single sight of Hunter. She'd resigned herself to the fact she'd never see him again. She certainly hadn't imagined he'd re-enter her life in such a crazy way. One minute, she was seconds away from walking down the aisle to be married and the next he had her slung over his shoulder, carrying her off to who knew where.

Shock held her hostage, keeping coherent thought from forming. She didn't understand what was happening. How in the world did he know she was getting married today? How did he know where to find her?

"Let me out of here," she demanded as he guided her car out of the parking lot and into the alley. "I'm not going anywhere but back inside the church."

He threw an arrogant smirk her way, winding around the trashcans littering the alley to the main street. She thought about screaming but knew it would be a waste of breath. There was little chance anyone would hear her. And even if they did, what good would it do?

Her only hope at getting away was trying to talk some sense into him. Hopefully, he still had some brains left inside that head of his. Fidgeting in her seat, she smoothed the creases in her gown as she fought back the confusion.

Turning to face him, she took a deep breath, erasing the anger from her voice. She'd try reasoning with him. Once he realized how crazy this was, he'd have to take her back to the church.

"In case the obvious didn't hit you, I was about to be married."

"I'm aware of that," he returned, never taking his eyes off the road ahead.

"Then don't you think it would be wise to take me back before someone realizes I'm gone?"

He didn't bother answering, only shrugged his

shoulders.

"Look, Hunter." She had to keep trying. "I don't know what you're up to. And truthfully, I don't want to know. All I care about is getting back to the church. If you take me back now, I promise this will all be forgotten."

He didn't answer, didn't even bother turning around. She scowled out the window as downtown passed by, leaving the church, her wedding, farther and farther behind.

By now, her father would have discovered she wasn't in her dressing room. It wouldn't be long before they figured out she wasn't inside the church and the search for the missing bride would begin. With nearly five hundred guests waiting for a wedding that had been talked about for months, they weren't going to give up easily. She was sure of it.

Unfortunately, if she couldn't convince Hunter to take her back, there wouldn't be a wedding. She could only imagine Grant's reaction. His public image meant so much. It wasn't going to make him happy to be embarrassed in front of all those guests. He'd see it as a black mark on the reputation he worked so hard to maintain.

"Please, Hunter." She tried a different tactic. If reason didn't get through, maybe pleading would. "Just turn around and take me back. You and I both know it's the smartest thing you can do."

"Sorry," he spared her a quick glance, "but we won't be going back. You can plead and beg or fight and scream. To me, it doesn't make a difference. You won't change my mind either way."

The fact he'd caught on to the different tactics

she'd been using irked her more than she cared to admit. At one time, he'd known her better than anyone, but those days were long gone. The last thing she wanted was a reminder of how close they had once been. It had taken too long to get him out of her system. She refused to struggle through such an ordeal again.

"Then at least have the decency of telling me what exactly it is you're up to. Or do you make it a habit of kidnapping brides from their weddings seconds before they're due to walk down the aisle?"

"You're my first." His deep voice vibrated inside the tight confines of the car. That voice used to slide over her skin like silk. At one time in her life, she'd craved the sound of it, spent her days hearing it repeated inside her head.

"Then why? Is this some sort of sick revenge?"

The chuckle he returned lacked any kind of humor. "Don't flatter yourself, princess. I don't have the time, or the want, to find revenge. It wouldn't be worth it."

His words hit painfully though she shouldn't have expected any less. Their parting hadn't been a friendly one. It left large, gaping holes in both of them. Holes she knew had never fully healed.

In one last jab of desperation, she glanced behind her. The church was no longer in sight. They'd slipped through the heart of the city, leaving the skyscrapers and crowded streets behind.

With that one last look, she'd lost all hope of getting back to her wedding. Whatever Hunter's plans were, they didn't include taking her back to the church. There wasn't going to be a wedding today. Of that, she was sure.

Fear was an emotion she should have had growing

inside. She had no idea what was going on inside Hunter's thick head. She didn't know why he'd come after her or where he was taking her.

Yet, something inside refused to be afraid of him. Even with his strange actions, he didn't frighten her. Worried, yes. Confused, even more so. But, even after all this time, she knew he wouldn't harm her. A small thread of trust continued to exist. A trust she hadn't been aware she still carried until now.

"All right." She fell into the passenger seat in a defeated slump. "If this isn't for revenge, then what's it for? I think I deserve some sort of explanation."

"And you'll get it." His eyes were hard and cold as they landed on her. "Later."

The man could be so infuriating. Paxton bit down hard on her bottom lip, stopping the words of frustration bubbling inside. Arguing with him would do no good. She'd already figured that much out. Right now, he called all the shots. It drove her crazy but there wasn't much she could do about it.

She wanted to ask him where they were going but figured it would be another question he refused to answer. He was an impenetrable wall, one she didn't have the strength to try breaking through.

Silence fell. Hunter guided the car onto the interstate, steering them toward the western skyline. The Rockies loomed ahead, high and mighty in their regal stance. Though summer was firmly in place, white patches of snow still covered the highest peaks, contrasting against the lush green below.

It was a breathtaking scene. One no picture could ever do justice. Doing her best to black out the man at her side, she concentrated on the scenery and tried letting the beauty wash away the anxious nerves jumping around inside.

Less than an hour later, they became a part of that scenery. Hunter expertly handled the road as the mountain climb began. The dark night blanketed over them, a deeper black in the mountains than it was in the city. The interstate loomed ahead with the glare of headlights breaking through the darkness.

She kept waiting for him to stop and turn off on one of the exits, but he showed no signs of slowing.

The hours crept by and with their passing exhaustion set in. The green glow of the dashboard clock read off the ten o'clock hour before he finally slowed to exit the interstate, turning onto a smaller highway cutting through the mountainside.

Paxton's eyes widened as she realized where the highway would take them. After many twists and turns, the road stretched through the middle of Willow Park. The small resort town cozily nestled in the heart of Pine Valley was one she knew well. Ten miles above the town, hidden away on its own private mountain, sat her grandfather's cabin.

At eighteen, wide-eyed and naïve, she'd taken a younger Hunter there. The emotions from what they'd shared that night still filled her heart. The memory was one she would carry with her for the rest of her life.

She glanced at Hunter. Did he remember? He had to. It was impossible to forget the passion burning like a wildfire between them. Yet, he showed no signs behind his stony expression. His eyes remained steadfast on the road ahead. His posture stayed as cool and collected as it had from the beginning.

If he noticed the tension at his side, he didn't show

it. How could he ignore the heated memories? They washed over her, relentless and demanding. The smallest thought of what happened was enough to bring a warm flush to her cheeks.

Her grandfather's cabin was the last place she wanted to be. The memories were too painful. They belonged buried in the past. Returning to the cabin would only dig them back up and bring back raw and painful images she wanted nothing to do with.

Chapter Two

Mitchell Walsh's cabin was far from the small, modest abode he'd first expected. Dark wood logs forming the outside wall were the only truth to the term cabin. The rest was something else altogether.

As he had the last time he visited, Hunter shook his head in disbelief. The two-story, sprawling structure in front of him was what the Walsh family referred to as their little getaway.

Heck, the apartment he lived in as a boy was only as big as one of the rooms inside. He'd never even imagined such places existed until he met Paxton. Until her, he'd never let himself think of how the other side lived. It was hard enough dealing with the way he had to live.

Tires ground against the pebble drive as the Cherokee rolled to a stop. Slamming the gearshift into park with more force than needed, he cursed his stupidity for coming here. What in the world had he been thinking?

He hadn't been thinking. That was the problem. Since the moment he stepped into that room, caught sight of Paxton, all rational thought flew out the window. What possessed him to do what he'd done? One minute he stood there, held in a daze by sapphire eyes warring with his, and the next he had Paxton slung over his shoulder, heading for the back door.

He didn't know how he'd managed to get away without being seen. Fate had worked to his advantage. Or maybe it had worked against him. It almost seemed too easy getting her out and away from the church.

There was one of two things happening. Either someone upstairs was looking out for him or someone down below had a very sick sense of humor.

"Can I trust you not to try anything stupid?" He looked at her through the shadows of the night.

He wasn't worried about her trying to get away. There wasn't anywhere to go. And if she did try, she didn't have much chance of out-running him.

"I think we've had enough stupidity for the day." She refused to look at him. Her hand was on the handle as soon as the locks released. Before he had a chance to climb out, she was already on her way to the front door. With a stiff spine and squared shoulders, it wasn't hard to read the anger roaring inside.

What did he care if she was angry? Hunter slammed the car door. He wasn't any happier about the situation. The last place he wanted to be was at this cabin with her. Too many memories came with the damn place. If he had it his way, he'd be back in his hotel room, watching the baseball game with a cold one.

Bad judgment had brought him here. After his little stunt back at the church, he had to get Paxton as far away from Denver as possible. The only logical place that came to mind was the cabin. It was remote, far removed from the city, and at least somewhat familiar to both of them.

It was only for one night. By tomorrow morning, Grant would be tucked safely behind bars and Paxton would be free to go. By then, it would be good riddance, as far as he was concerned.

The sooner he was rid of her, the better.

"How do you plan to get in?" Disgust darkened her gaze as he joined her on the front porch. She folded her arms tight over her wrinkled gown, her sandaled toe beating an impatient rhythm on the wooden boards below. "I certainly hope you don't plan on breaking in. I would think you've broken the law enough for one day."

"I haven't broken any laws." He reached over her head. Running his hands along the molding over the door, he located the key in a matter of seconds. "And I don't plan on starting now."

Even after ten years, the Walsh family was as predictable as ever. Paxton still left her car keys hidden in the sun visor, and the spare key to the cabin was still in the exact spot it had been the last time he was here.

She scowled when he reached around her, shoving the door open. The bare skin of her back rubbed against his chest as she scooted past.

His pulse quickened. Angry she could still get to him, he slammed the door, earning an irritated glare from the princess.

"I'm going to brew a pot of coffee and then I expect an explanation." She stormed toward the kitchen without giving him a chance to respond. From the front hallway, he listened as cupboards squeaked open then slammed shut. Obviously, she hadn't grown out of her hot-blooded temper.

Knowing better than to bother her in such a mood, he settled in the breakfast nook. Floor to ceiling windows provided an unobstructed view of the wilderness surrounding the cabin. During daylight it was a magnificent view. One he and Paxton had enjoyed after a night of heated passion.

She'd sat on his lap, head resting on his shoulder, her fresh scent washing over him. Her lips had been swollen from a long night of his kisses. Cheeks stained bright red, she'd been the symbol of beauty. A sight more breathtaking than what nature provided outside the windows. He'd wanted her so bad then. Wanted to take her in his arms and—

Damn. He cut off the direction of his wandering thoughts before they flew out of control. The past was the past. That's where it was going to stay. He had neither the patience nor the desire to bring up memories better left forgotten.

"All right, Hunter, spill your guts." Paxton stepped into the breakfast nook holding two ceramic mugs, steam rolling over the rims.

She sat one mug in front of him. Claiming the chair across the table, she settled with her own mug.

"It's been ten years since we last saw one another," she supplied as if he didn't already know. "Ten years then suddenly you appear on the day of my wedding and haul me away before I have a chance to take a single step down the aisle."

"Thanks for recapping that for me." He earned a hard stare from across the table.

"I want an explanation, Hunter. I deserve an explanation."

He couldn't argue. Sitting across from him in a wrinkled gown of white lace, errant strands of honey-blond hair circling her face, she looked somewhat misplaced. A lost bride in search of answers. Her sapphire eyes spoke their own questions. Their deep blue color darkened as she attempted to peek into his thoughts for some grasp of reason.

Deliberately taking his time, he took a long drink of coffee. Resting back in his chair, he stretched his long legs in front of him. Impatience rained over Paxton's face. She shot him a look of warning. Pulling up straight in her chair, she squared off with him across the length of the table.

"How long have you been engaged to Grant Robinson?"

"What does that have to do with anything?" She shook her head and folded her arms defiantly over her full breasts.

"How long?" He felt his anger rising but pushed it down as he set his mug down with more force than necessary.

"Six months." Anger brewed heavy in her voice. "And we've been dating for almost a year."

Hunter pushed his chair back onto two legs and crossed his arms loosely over his chest. "The Bureau has had their eyes on him for a lot longer. He isn't exactly an upstanding citizen. He's considered one of our most wanted criminals."

"Grant, a criminal." Her voice hovered close to a yell. "I think you have your wires crossed somewhere. The Grant Robinson I know is anything but a criminal."

"Then you must not know the guy all that well." He thought of what he'd learned about the case. The guy had to have been good to fool Paxton.

"Look, Hunter." She leaned over the table, shortening the distance between them. "I'm not exactly sure what you're trying to prove. But you're never going to convince me Grant is involved in anything illegal. I would know if he was, trust me."

He set his chair back down on all four legs with a loud thud. Wrapping his hands around the heated sides of his mug, he stared hard into her sapphire eyes. "I don't suppose you noticed a few uninvited guests at your wedding this afternoon."

"I never had a chance to see any of the guests." She shot him a dirty look. "You made sure of that."

"What I made sure of was saving you from being hauled in for questioning while your fiancé was being taken into custody."

Across from him, Paxton's mouth fell open.

"Your romantic wedding night would have been spent inside a windowless room with some overworked agent pounding you for information."

He dropped his hands from the mug and crossed his arms over his chest again. A knowing smirk spread over his lips. "Think what the papers would look like tomorrow morning—*Paxton Walsh taken in for questioning.* I can only imagine the rumors that would fly after that little tidbit was released. Especially when it came out you married a man who is bound to spend the rest of his life behind bars."

Her gaping mouth snapped shut. The air around them grew thick and heavy as she caught him with a hard, blank stare. He held his patience as he waited for her reaction. He saw it brewing as heat rose off her, staining her cheeks a bright, crimson red. He had no idea what to expect, but he was prepared for just about anything.

It wasn't every day someone learned the person they were going to marry was a hard-worn criminal.

Though he no longer cared about her, he was willing to offer comfort while the truth settled. He'd forget the bitterness between them long enough to provide his shoulder for her to cry on.

"I can't believe this." Her voice escaped barely above a whisper.

He nodded, waiting for the fall out. "I'm sure it's difficult coming to terms with."

Blazing eyes met his. "What's difficult coming to terms with is the fact you'd fabricate such a lie."

"A lie?" Surprise nearly knocked him off his chair.

"Of all the nerve." Paxton shot up from her seat, tumbling the chair behind her. "You, Hunter Reese, are an insufferable, annoying jerk. You ruin my wedding day then come up with this crazy tale to cover yourself. Like I wouldn't be able to see straight through you."

He bolted from his chair, facing her down. A good six inches taller, he hovered over her, staring down into a face that looked ready to kill. Good, he was ready for a fight.

"I don't lie." He moved around the table and took a threatening step closer. To her credit, she didn't back down. She stood solid where she was, showing no signs of retreat. "I could care less whether you believe me or not. I've told you the truth. I'm not about to stand around and defend myself for doing so."

"I risked my butt getting you away from Grant before you were dragged into the mess he created." A blaze of angry fire roared to life inside. "I could lose my badge for this. They don't take kindly to agents stealing away with a possible suspect."

"You risked your badge and your butt for your own crazy reasons. Don't blame me. It's not my fault you have some sort of sick revenge eating away inside."

"Is that what you think?" He loomed over her. "You think I did this because I want to get back at you?"

"Why not?" She shrugged, ready for a struggle. "It's the only reason that makes sense. It probably gave you a thrill to ruin the biggest day of my life."

"What would give me a thrill would be to take you straight back to that damn church and make you face the music alone." He ran an aggravated hand through his hair. "What in the world was I thinking, trying to help you. I should have known you'd be as ungrateful as ever."

"What do I have to be grateful for? The fact you ruined my wedding? Or that I'm stuck with you in this stupid cabin when you're the last person I want to spend time with."

"The feeling is mutual, princess. You aren't exactly my first choice for a companion either."

"Then take me home." A touch of desperation echoed in her words. "I don't think either of us is going to be too deeply hurt if you do."

"First thing tomorrow morning, I plan to do just that." He ignored the desperation, refusing to let it sway him. "And when you find out your precious fiancé is locked safely behind bars, maybe you'll see who's not thinking rationally around here."

"Fine." She glared at him, her temper hot in her fiery gaze.

It matched the same temper burning through his veins. "Fine."

They stared at each other, neither willing to be the first to back down. Every muscle inside Hunter's body tensed. Barely tempered heat simmered between them, feeding the raging emotions burning inside. Gray eyes battled with blue as stubborn wills emerged to fight.

He stood close enough to see her pulse flutter in her neck and the heavy rise and fall of her chest with each breath. She didn't flinch under his heavy gaze, instead, she stood strong and sturdy, daring him with her eyes.

It took all his strength not to reach out and place a punishing kiss on those full lips. His hands itched to grab her. His body hardened with a need to show her who was in charge. He had no doubt he could erase the smug look from her face. He still remembered what his touch could do. He could bring her crumbling to her feet in mere seconds if he wanted to.

And that was the problem. He did want to. Beyond the anger, beyond the rage, he wanted nothing more than to feel Paxton's body melt under his touch. He wanted to taste those lips of hers and see if they were still as sweet as he remembered. Desire raged inside, fighting with his stumbling control.

His hands turned to fists at his sides. "Go to bed, Paxton."

Her mouth opened then closed. Her stance faltered. Apparently, she saw the desire etched in the lines of his face. He struggled for the last thread of control, holding on as if it was his lifeline.

"Go."

Pivoting on the balls of her feet, she spun away, honey-blond hair feathering against his rough cheeks. She stormed down the hall, turning sharply for the stairs, leaving only the gentle scent of her perfume behind.

Once she was no longer in sight, he turned back to the table. Grabbing his lukewarm coffee, he made a straight line for the back door. A cold blast of mountain air would do him good right about now.

A chilled breeze slapped against him as he stepped out onto the back porch. The night was pitch black without lights breaking through the darkness. Somewhere off in the distance, he heard the flutter of an animal sweeping through the trees, holding a night vision he could only wish for.

Slowly his muscles uncoiled as his breathing returned to normal. The rapid beat of his heart slowed inside his chest until he no longer noticed its rhythm. Control again simmered over him, settling deep into his bones, taking over where chaos had once reigned.

He was an idiot. It was as plain and simple as that. He was a man trained to think before he acted. Programmed never to let his emotions rule. Yet today, every bit of those qualities had taken a leave of absence. He'd acted rashly, without thought, letting old feelings take over.

An idiot.

He took a large swallow of the tepid black liquid sloshing around inside of his mug. The bitter taste washed down his throat, settling like a rock inside his stomach. From above, a light filtered out the window, creating dim shadows along the ground below.

Paxton. The name ran through his mind. Damn that woman for what she did to him. Inside his memories, he'd carried the portrait of a young, shimmering teenage girl who had stolen his heart with the first glance. He'd kept it with him for years, never changing, never altering, that image.

Now another image clouded his thoughts. She was beautiful when she was younger, but she'd matured right into breathtaking. Her body curved seductively in all the right places, reminding him he was no longer dealing with a young girl, but with a woman. A very mature, very alluring woman.

He'd been an utter fool ten years ago, trapped by her beauty. At eighteen, she'd already become seductive, tempting him with nothing more than a mere glance from those sapphire eyes surrounded by long lashes. She had him wrapped around her little finger, completely lost in her promises of love.

He'd believed her back then. Had actually thought seriously about marrying her. There was nothing he wouldn't have given her. Nothing he wouldn't have done for her. She'd taken all he offered then shattered any hopes and dreams he may have carried. With little more than a backward glance, she'd walked away, leaving him broken and humiliated.

She taught him a rough lesson about life. Dreams were for fools. Love was for idiots. He'd picked himself up, hardened his heart against any more pain, and carried on with his life. He swore many times he'd never make the same mistake again. And until now, he'd kept that promise.

The light disappeared and Hunter figured she'd retired for the night. Turning back to the cabin, he knew it was best for him to do the same. He could beat himself up all night, it wouldn't do any good. So he had slipped. Everyone was entitled to at least one setback. He knew better now. There wouldn't be a second time.

Upstairs, he hitched his hands around the back of the most comfortable looking chair he could find. Using the last of his strength, he hoisted it off the floor and carried it to the closed door where he knew Paxton slept. Until tomorrow morning, like it or not, she was his responsibility. He wasn't about to take any chances.

It was just one night. It wasn't going to kill him. Tomorrow he'd be free of her and this little mishap in his life would be long forgotten.

****

At least she had a familiar bed to sleep in. Paxton twisted uncomfortably underneath the crisp, white sheets. Her limbs ached. Her bare skin burned. She'd been fine, just fine, until Hunter had gone and changed the boundaries without warning. She could spar with the man easily. Could even get into a knock down drag out fight and still come out okay. But when it came to warring against the desire that used to blaze between them, she was completely unprepared.

That look. That heated, uncontrolled look burning in his eyes. It was one she knew all too well. One still etched deep in her mind. She'd known instantly what he wanted. It had frightened her even as it sent a familiar thrill of excitement shooting through.

Black hair, gray eyed, Hunter Reese. His dark sensuality had lapped at her senses relentlessly when she was a naïve teenager.

She'd grown out of that stage, never expecting she'd have to face down an even more virile and stunning man ten years later. Hard, corded muscles had formed where once there had been none. A face, once boyishly sexy, now screamed with masculine dignity.

He was much more than she remembered. More of a man, hard and firm in all the right places. And more of a threat with those alluring gray eyes lashing a hole straight through to her soul. He was harder, more reserved, giving him a mysterious quality that was enticing as well as unsettling.

She smothered her face with a pillow. She didn't want to think about him. Had no right to think about him. She should be thinking about Grant who was probably frantic to know where his wife-to-be had disappeared to.

Tossing a limp arm over the side of the mattress, she turned her head, staring at the wrinkled gown crumpled on the floor. This wasn't how she planned to spend this night. It was far from what she expected. Hunter, with his far-fetched cloak and dagger tale, had put a damper on all her plans.

His words drifted through her mind, sounding just as ridiculous the second time around. So what if she'd experienced doubts about Grant. Just because she had an occasion to wonder what secrets he kept didn't mean anything Hunter said was true. She'd know if Grant was involved in anything even the least bit illegal. Doubts and questions on her part didn't make him into the criminal Hunter portrayed him to be.

Tomorrow.

She clung to that one single word. Tomorrow, the nightmare would be over. Hunter would be gone, and she'd be back with Grant where she belonged.

"Tomorrow," the word slipped quietly off her lips as she drifted to sleep.

Chapter Three

He felt as old and creaky as the chair he sat in. Stretching his legs, Hunter was thankful this would all be over in a couple of hours. He'd have questions to answer when he got back to Denver, but the worst of it would be done as soon as he returned Paxton to where she belonged.

The hinges of the door creaked. He turned his head and caught her stepping out of the room.

His eyes strayed to the scrap of white silk barely covering her luscious body. Her breasts peeked over the sinfully thin strip of lingerie. Skin shadowed through the silk, giving more than a hint to what lay underneath.

His long, lingering gaze swept over her. Even the strongest of men couldn't resist the temptation she offered. His aching muscles forgotten, a rapid tightening clenched every inch of his body. Old, forgotten needs zipped to life, breaking through the barriers he'd carefully constructed.

"Morning," he drawled, never letting his gaze wander.

She flustered at the sound of his voice. Shock, from the unexpected sight of him, registered quickly. Her arms flying around her middle, she did what little she could to cover up. But it was too late. He'd already been given an eye-full.

"What are you doing there?" She tugged uselessly

at the lace, hiding nothing.

"My bed." He swept his hand around the chair, enjoying the view from his position.

"You slept there all night?"

Nodding, he stood, bringing him within inches of where she'd stopped. Close enough to watch as goose bumps formed on her skin.

"There are plenty of rooms you could have stayed in." She shifted awkwardly on bare feet. Her eyes flew to the bathroom door.

"So there are." His thoughts weren't on where the beds were located. The only bed he cared about, at the moment, was whatever one he might find her in.

"Have you had enough?"

Her voice drew his attention back to her face. She glared at him through hovering lids, pulling her pouty lips into a tight, furious line.

"What?" He stumbled to regain control. It should be illegal for a woman to look as good as she did standing in front of him, half-naked.

"You're practically drooling." She shook her head in disgust. Scooting around him, she headed for the bathroom.

"For the record," she shot over her shoulder before disappearing behind the door. "I wore this for Grant's eyes. Not yours."

A cold shower couldn't have worked any faster bringing him back to reality. He landed with a painful thud as the bathroom door slammed closed. Enough was enough. It was time to get rid of the irritating thorn in his side so he could get on with more important things.

His heavy footsteps echoed through the hall. At the

stairs, he heard the shower kick on behind the bathroom door. He paused for a moment as images of Paxton's naked body under the streaming water came to life. As quickly as they formed, he pushed them away.

What he wouldn't give to be able to go back in time. Twenty-four hours was all he needed. That would be more than enough to right the wrongs he'd committed. He should have known better than to get within even twenty miles of Paxton. Past experiences should have warned him away.

Trudging down the stairs, he cursed his old protective instinct for her. She was not his concern. If she was dumb enough to agree to marry a man like Grant, then she deserved to live through the questioning the Bureau had planned.

He should have left her alone. Should have taken himself off the case in the beginning and hightailed it back to Washington.

Reaching the kitchen, he started a pot of coffee before digging his phone from his pocket. His fingers hit the small buttons hard, releasing some of the tension building up in his shoulders and spine.

On the fourth ring, his partner's familiar voice completed the connection.

"Reese, where in the hell are you?" Smith's deep voice boomed. "Williams is having a fit. He's been trying to contact you since yesterday afternoon."

"It's a long story. I'll explain when I get there."

"You'd better get here soon. We've got ourselves a mess. Williams wants every agent reporting within the hour."

He rested a hip up against the edge of the counter. He knew he wasn't going to like what he was about to hear. Sucking in a harsh breath, he fought off the headache threatening to take shape in his right temple. "What's the bad news?"

"Grant Robinson is a free man."

The statement fell like a cement slab inside his gut. "What happened? I thought we had him wrapped up nice and tight."

Smith's sigh was harsh. "We did, until we found our informant with a bullet hole through his head. The agents who were on his watch are gone too."

He bit back the nasty word threatening to escape. He knew the agents who'd been assigned to watch over their informant. Good guys, they both were, with families waiting for them back home. "Was Grant taken into custody?"

"Nope." Smith's tone was harsh. "Orders came that we were to leave him be before anyone got a hand on him."

Hunter shoved away from the counter, stopping long enough to pour himself a cup of coffee before pacing back and forth across the kitchen floor.

"That's not all of it." Frustration was clear as it poured through the line. "Not only did Grant walk away, but his bride-to-be disappeared before the ceremony. Not one of our people spotted her. She pretty much disappeared into thin air."

He paused. "How did Grant take that?"

"Don't know. But there's a rumor flying around he's got some of his men looking for her. Of course, nothing can be confirmed."

Of course. Hunter's restless pacing picked up again. Nothing about Grant could ever be confirmed, that was the problem. The Bureau only had those flying rumors to go on. It was irritating as well as frustrating.

"What's your take on why he has his men on the hunt for his missing bride?" He hoped his partner's theory didn't match his own.

"Personally, I think the guy's worried, afraid she found out about him and has some germ of evidence that could take him down. Seems to me, he's probably a bit nervous as to why she changed her mind at the last minute."

That was what he didn't want to hear. He'd come up with the same suspicions. His little stunt yesterday afternoon had inadvertently put Paxton in jeopardy. Instead of saving her from the questioning, he'd stuck her right in the middle of danger. "I need you to do me a couple favors."

From above, the sound of Paxton's shower ended. He knew he needed to end the call. He had some explaining to do when she appeared.

"I'll do what I can."

Hunter sauntered over to the window and looked out over the trees climbing up the side of the mountain. This was it. His job was on the line. He knew what he had to do. "Let Williams know I won't be reporting today."

"That's not going to make him happy. He already has a score to settle with you because of your sudden disappearance."

"I know, but that will have to wait. There's a more pressing matter at hand. You'll also have to inform him I'm officially going on protective duty."

"Protective duty?" Confusion was clear in his partner's words. "What in the world for?"

Hunter pinched the bridge of his nose, fighting off

the headache. "Because Paxton is with me and we both know what Grant wants from her."

Smith let out a low whistle. "Boy, you really know how to get your butt in a sling. Williams is going to be biting nails when I tell him."

Outside, a Robin bounced from branch to branch. What he wouldn't have given to be able to trade places with him. "I know, but I don't have any other choice. Paxton is in danger because of me. It's my responsibility to make sure nothing happens to her."

"Do I even want to know how she wound up with you?"

"It's a long story," Hunter sighed. "Just let Williams know what's going on. I'll check back with you later."

He ended the call, shoving his phone back in his pocket. Refreshing his coffee, he settled at the kitchen table and prepared for another battle with Paxton.

****

The shower left her skin red and burning. She'd turned the temperature up almost as high as it could go, hoping to wash away the feel of Hunter's eyes scouring over her.

It hadn't done any good. She still felt the sizzle of those dark gray eyes taking her in.

This wasn't how it was supposed to be. Her life was in order. She'd set it in a direction carefully planned. Ten years ago she'd made a decision that had separated her from Hunter and had spent every day since finding her way without him in her life.

Foolishly, she'd believed agreeing to marry Grant had been the last step in erasing Hunter from her life. She'd been so sure she was over him. Until this morning when her reaction to his burning gaze shattered all she'd worked so hard to accomplish.

He still held a power over her. The thought terrified her. She never wanted to relive what had happened on the day she'd told him goodbye. The pain was too great. The heartache too fierce. The decisions she'd made back then had been the hardest ones of her life. To completely shut him out had almost killed her, but she'd done it—for him.

Peeking around the corner of the bathroom door, she made sure the coast was clear before venturing into the hallway in nothing more than a white, cotton towel. In seconds, she was back inside the safety of her bedroom, rummaging through the dresser drawers.

Getting away from Hunter was the only way to protect herself. She had to get away before her heart remembered what they once shared. Before her soul began craving his existence all over again.

Dressed in a pair of denim shorts and a red cotton shirt, she headed downstairs. She only had to face the ride home then she'd be done. The thought didn't offer as much relief as she'd hoped. Some small part inside called out in disappointment.

It only proved how desperately she needed him out of her life. The more distance between them, the better. She had a fiancé to go home to, volunteer work waiting, and a wedding to reschedule. There were plenty of things to keep her busy and make her forget this forbidden slice in time with Hunter.

She found him sitting at the kitchen table, staring out the window. Outside, sunlight streamed through the long branches, crystallizing on the morning dew. A lone rabbit positioned itself at the edge of the forest line, glancing back and forth between the cabin and the mountain behind him.

At any other time, she'd be reluctant to leave. She loved her grandfather's cabin. Loved the peace and tranquility it offered. That was why she'd first brought Hunter here, to share the beauty with him and be part of this special place.

"I made coffee," he informed her as her footsteps reached him.

Moving closer, she picked up on small things she missed before. He sat at the table, broad shoulders slumped forward. A look of defeat clouded his expression. So used to the strong, virile man he usually was, she worried about the changes.

Pouring a cup of coffee, she joined him at the table. He didn't turn to face her. His attention stayed glued to the window. She had a feeling he wasn't seeing anything. There was a blank look in his eyes, registering little of his surroundings.

"Well," she began after her first sip of coffee. "Are you about ready to go?"

Slowly, he looked at her. He said nothing, leaving her wondering. When his mouth did open to speak, a low grumble escaped.

"There's been a change of plans. We aren't going anywhere."

Chapter Four

"What do you mean we aren't going anywhere?" Paxton slammed her coffee cup on the table, black liquid spilling over the sides. "You said this nightmare would be over."

"I was wrong."

"You were wrong." Anger echoed in her voice. "What exactly do you mean by that?"

"Just what I said." He barely spared her a glance. "I was wrong. We aren't going anywhere, least of all back to Denver."

"Don't do this, Hunter." She pushed from her seat. Hands on her hips, she glared down at where he continued to sit. Calm. Sipping at his coffee. "You can't want me around anymore than I want to be with you. Why don't you end the torture before it gets any worse?"

There was a sharp cut to his gaze as he looked at her. "I would like nothing more than to do that, but your fiancé has left me no choice."

She shook her head, falling back into her seat. She didn't want to hear any more of his silly stories about Grant. She'd gotten her fill yesterday. "What does Grant have to do with this?"

"He made sure the Bureau had no ties to bring him in by having our informant and two of our agents killed." There was a sadness in his eyes she refused to acknowledge.

"So now you're telling me Grant is a killer. And here I thought what you told me last night was hard to believe."

He rose from his chair. In two steps, he stood over her, dark eyes boring into hers. She clenched her hands at her sides, trying not to squirm under his stare.

"Believe this, when you didn't walk down that aisle yesterday, Grant got worried."

"Of course he was worried." She struggled to hold on to what patience she had left. "I disappeared without a word."

Reaching out, he gripped her chin between his rough fingers, tilting her face to his. "It's not your wellbeing he's worried about, princess. It's his own."

She yanked free, the warmth of his large fingers against her skin affecting her more than she cared to admit. A tremor drifted up her spine as his touch lingered even after his hand fell away.

He turned, taking a place in front of the window. Clasping his hands behind his back, he kept his attention on the lush wilderness outside. "My guess is, Grant suspects you found some dirt on him so you stood him up at the altar."

"But I didn't stand him up." She wished he'd turn around so she didn't have to speak to his back. "If it weren't for you, I'd be a married woman right now."

"Well…now you're a hunted woman."

"Enough." She slammed open palms against the table and shoved out of her chair. "First, you want me to believe Grant is some awful criminal, and he's a killer. Now you want me to believe he's after me."

She stormed to his side, caring little about his lack

of attention. She didn't care if he looked at her or not. He was going to listen until she convinced him to give up on this stupid game of his.

Maybe he was delusional, sick in the head. Maybe that was why he came up with such fairy tales. Too many years dealing with his kind of work could have caused complications, making him believe things that weren't true.

She didn't know what it was. Didn't care. All she wanted was to get out of here. He'd gone too far, kidnapping her then filling her head with lies. It was time to put an end to it before things got worse.

"Look, Hunter." She fought to keep her voice steady. "Either you take me back to Denver yourself or I'll do it on my own. I don't need you to get me back. I'm perfectly capable of going on my own."

"You won't get the keys, and it's a long walk back."

Paxton bit down on her temper. "Then I'll call my father or Grant to pick me up." She thought of her cell phone back in the church's dressing room, suddenly thankful the cabin still had a land line. "It might take longer than I hoped, but I'm not against the wait."

He turned away from the window. His hard, cold expression ran a chill through her veins. She wasn't sure what to expect. She wanted to believe he'd come to his senses and agree to take her back to Denver, or at least give her the keys so she could drive herself. But there was no reading a man like him. Whatever his feelings were, he kept them locked tightly behind his stony façade.

"So what's it going to be? Do we head back to Denver or do I call my father?"

Hunter's eyes strayed, finding the telephone between him and the wall. "To get to the phone, you'll have to go through me first."

"Don't threaten me." She shoved her hands on her hips, refusing to back down. He could fight with all he had, she wasn't going to let him intimidate her.

"That's not a threat, princess. It's a promise."

The man was the most insufferable, irritating creature alive. She wasn't one who believed in violence. But, at the moment, she wanted nothing more than to wring his neck.

If he thought he could scare her into giving up, he was wrong. He might have won the first round, but she still had plenty of fight left in her. "I'm going upstairs before I do or say something I might regret, but this is far from over. I will be going home. With you or without you."

Without waiting for a reply, she stormed away. Her blood boiled. Her face burned. She had never been so angry with anyone in her entire life. If she didn't distance herself, there was no telling what she might do. Her mind formed vivid images of how she could take her building frustration out on him.

She took the stairs two at a time. He thought he was in control, but she wasn't about to let that be the case. If he wouldn't give in on his own, she'd simply wait until his guard was down. It would be easy enough to get to the telephone when his back was turned.

And if that didn't come through for her, she'd wait for a chance to break away on her own. It was a walk, but she could make it into Willow Park if she pushed herself. From there, she'd call her father or Grant to pick her up.

She slammed the door of her bedroom, smiling in satisfaction as it rattled the walls, echoed through the house. She wasn't going to be a prisoner to Hunter. She had a father and a fiancé who had to be worried sick. Getting back to them was her only concern. If it meant out-tricking Hunter at his own game, then so be it.

****

Hunter couldn't help the smile sneaking across his face as the door slammed above. Paxton's red-hot temper had always fascinated him. Her eyes sparked a deep heat when fury raged inside. She was a spitfire when she was in this kind of mood. A hurricane of fire and brimstone boiling to the surface.

He still remembered the first time her temper had erupted. Only a month into their relationship, he'd made the mistake of telling her she didn't know what hardship was coming from her privileged life. Those eyes of hers had flared as she told him how wrong he was. She'd lost her mother at only five years old, leaving her to be raised by a father who thought he controlled every little part of her life.

She made him see she'd had her own struggles. She may not have known the hardness of poverty the way he had, but her problems had been just as real, growing up in a house where reputation was everything. Where more emphasis was placed on how you presented yourself to the outside world than on how you acted behind closed doors.

He hadn't blamed her for being angry then, and he couldn't blame her now. It was his fault she was stuck in this mess. His fault she couldn't go home where she wanted to be.

Grabbing her empty coffee cup along with his own,

he made his way to the kitchen sink. Turning the taps, warm water rushed over his hands as he rinsed out the mugs.

Heavy footfalls echoed in the ceiling above. He pictured her pacing the floor—hands clenched behind her back while she cursed him and all that he was.

He'd let her cool her heels for the time being. It would do them both some good. Then maybe she'd finally be willing to listen to reason. Eventually, she was going to have to come to the realization everything he told her was truth.

Placing the coffee cups on a small towel, he reached for the outdated telephone, still corded, hanging on the wall. Thankfully, this was the only one in the cabin. Still, he didn't intend to plant himself in front of it all day, making sure Paxton didn't carry out her threat.

Lifting the receiver from its cradle, he disconnected it from the coiled cord. It dangled against the wall as he palmed the receiver and headed outside.

The sun warmed the mountain air, bringing forth a fresh scent of pine and timber. Stepping off the back porch, he covered the open space between the cabin and tree line. Reaching the edge of the forest, he held the receiver high in the air. With one long toss, he threw it into the thick span of trees.

Satisfied, he turned back for the house. The summer sun was warm on his shoulders. He couldn't bring himself to go inside yet. Hooking a hip against the wooden railing of the porch, the mechanics of his mind took over.

He knew he didn't have long at the cabin. If memory served him right, they only had a few days until the old couple who took care of the place showed up. And if not them, Grant was bound to search the cabin at some point.

Their time was limited. They could take the night, but tomorrow morning he'd have to get them back on the road. If he was lucky, it wouldn't be long before they found some kind of evidence to hang Grant on. In just twenty-four hours, Paxton was already testing every ounce of his patience. He wasn't sure how much more he could take.

****

The man was impossible.

Standing at the window, watching as evening fell around the cabin, Paxton let out a long, irritated sigh.

She thought she had one on him. Had finally fooled him at his own game. But he again took the upper hand, leaving her feeling like a fool as she'd stared at the dismembered telephone.

All day she'd waited for her chance, listening to every sound he made moving through the cabin. When he settled in the front room, his attention diverted by the magazine he flipped through, she took her chance.

His answering laughter filled the kitchen and followed her up the stairs. He thought he was clever, but she'd show him. No one held her against her will. Not even Hunter. She was only on strike one. She still had two more to go.

"Dinner's served." The deep rumble of his voice filtered through the door.

It was on the tip of her tongue to tell him what he could do with his dinner. But the rumbling of her stomach choked down the words. There was no reason to starve herself. Besides, it was her family's food he cooked. He was just lucky Rosita and Paul kept the cupboards well stocked.

Opening the door, she found he'd already returned to the kitchen. The hearty aroma of dinner drifted up, tickled her senses, sending another hungry rumble through her stomach.

He stood at the stove, his broad back facing her. Lean muscles pressed against his shirt as he stirred the food. Black hair brushed his collar as he rolled his shoulders back, setting the spoon on the counter beside him.

She remembered the feel of his hair falling through her fingers. She'd loved running her hands through it.

How many nights had they laid together in one another's embrace while she smoothed the strands from his face? It had been longer back then, hanging past his shoulders. And he'd taken to the habit of catching it at the back of his neck with a leather band.

He'd been a true rebel. Hard and defensive. He'd told her he learned to be tough at an early age, for survival on the streets where he grew up. With a drunken mother, an unknown father, he had no choice but to learn to protect himself.

Her heart had ached for him, for the small boy he'd been. She understood he used his hard front as a means to ward off any threats of pain, but she'd seen through it. One hard look and she discovered the real Hunter beneath his rough shell.

He did care though he was loath to admit it. He cared enough to want to make the streets different for the generations following him. That was why he chose law enforcement. Even back then, at barely twenty-one, he knew what it was he wanted. His goals were set, and he wasn't letting anything stand in his way.

It was for that reason she'd made her difficult decision, even though she'd known it would tear them both apart.

"If you're waiting to be served, you're wasting your time."

His deep growl tugged her from her thoughts.

"What?" The fog from the past slowly cleared away.

"I said, if you're waiting to be served then you're wasting your time. I'm sorry, but there aren't any servants here to tend to your needs."

She shot him the dirtiest look she could muster up. He believed her to be the same woman she'd been when they first met, materialistic and naïve. Didn't he realize people changed over time? He certainly had.

It was on the tip of her tongue to tell him she hadn't had a servant waiting on her in years. That her small bungalow housed only her, no one else. What would he say if he found out she took care of herself, cleaned up her own messes? She'd actually learned to cook decent meals over the years and was independent now. The way she always wanted to be.

But what did she care what he knew? He had no place in her future. That place was reserved for Grant. Turning away, grabbing a bowl for her stew, she tried centering her focus on an image of Grant but she couldn't do it.

Frustrated, she clenched her teeth, willing herself to bring her fiancé to mind. It had only been a day since she'd seen him last. Why was she having such a hard time?

She slammed the cupboard door with more force

than necessary when still no images came. Spinning on her heels, she found Hunter watching her with questioning eyes.

"What?" She took her frustration out on him. Pushing past, her shoulder brushing against his hard chest, she made her way to the stove.

"Something wrong?" He shot her an obnoxious grin as she shoveled stew into her bowl. Ignoring him, she dropped the ladle back into the pot, splashes of stew kicking out, staining the white porcelain.

His gray eyes followed her across the kitchen to the table. Sitting down, she started on her dinner as the heat of his gaze bore into her side. A shiver ran up her spine and through the fingers holding her spoon, causing it to clatter into her bowl.

"Nothing's wrong." She gave in, met his heavy gaze. "I'm just testy from being held here against my will. If you'd let me go, I'd be fine."

He mumbled something that sounded an awful lot like, *stubborn-headed woman*, before turning to the stove, dishing up his own dinner. By the time he joined her at the table, she was already halfway through her stew.

"You're going to make yourself sick." He took a bite from his own bowl.

"It's better than sitting too long with you," she snapped, but slowed down just the same. She really didn't want to be sick. Wouldn't that just add to the excitement?

"Well, while you're here with me, we need to discuss a few things."

"I don't have anything to discuss with you unless it involves leaving." She was losing her final hold on control. She only wanted to be done, away from Hunter.

"Actually it does."

The comment surprised her. Maybe he'd come to his senses. "Really?"

He nodded. "Tomorrow morning, bright and early, we head out."

"I'm so glad you've decided to take me back. I was afraid you were going to carry on with this game forever. I was getting worried—"

His hand shot up. "We're not going back to Denver."

She shook her head, trying to make sense of what was being said. "You said we were leaving."

"We are. We aren't safe here. Sooner or later, Grant is going to think to look for you here."

A painful throb pounded against her temples. She bit down on her lip, fighting off the upcoming headache. She couldn't carry on this same old fight with him. It was wearing her thin and taking a toll on her sanity. Arguing with him didn't do any good. He was as hard-headed as a rock.

She shook her head when he opened his mouth. "I don't want to hear it." Her voice was weak, tired. "I don't want to hear one more word about Grant, the FBI, or their questioning. Unless you're going to tell me you've given in and are taking me home, don't talk to me."

He shrugged, turning back to his stew. The rest of dinner passed by in silence. Their eyes never met as they finished their food then rinsed out their dishes.

She started up the stairs as soon as she could, never looking back. She wasn't sure what made her angrier, the fact he insisted on continuing with his wild story or, after being with him for such a short period, she wasn't able to bring a single image of Grant to mind.

She didn't want, or need, the reminder of what he once meant to her. Her heart had never fully recovered from telling him goodbye. His reappearance in her life caused large wounds to break open all over again.

He'd completed her at one point in her life. He'd been the missing piece her soul needed. She'd known everything about him back then, every little quirk he had.

The passion between them had been like no other. So intense it frightened her at times. She'd felt so empty, alone, when he was no longer there to share her days. She'd struggled through months, years, of healing. During that dark time in her life, she'd come to realize she'd depended too much on Hunter. She'd given too much of herself she could never get back. He was the reason breath left her lungs and her heart beat day after day.

It was after that she swore she'd never again let another man take over the way he had. She'd always kept a part of her heart out of Grant's reach, fearful she might never get it back. It had happened with Hunter, and she refused to repeat her mistakes.

Closing the door of her bedroom, she collapsed onto the bed. Unseeing eyes stared up at the stark white ceiling.

Hunter had done more than ruin her wedding day. Done more than she could begin to grasp. Even in her anger, she couldn't deny what was inside. Couldn't deny the doors trying to open again. He brought a hope she never thought she'd find. A foolish hope of again experiencing the special love they had once shared.

Chapter Five

She must have fallen asleep.

Paxton opened her eyes to a room dark under the cover of night. She'd worked herself into a tangled mess in the crisp, white sheets. Her face was hot. Her heart beat a mile a minute.

It was the dream. So real she still felt it.

Sitting up, she wrapped her arms around her bent legs, resting her chin against her knees. In sleep, she'd been making love to Hunter. The passion between them as fierce as it had ever been. They came together as one with bodies in perfect tune, needs never fully satisfied.

The dream had been so real. So alive. She'd thrived on his every move, craving his mere presence. Her love for him had been so strong, overwhelming.

Unable to escape the hold of it, she rolled off the bed and headed for the window. Crossing her arms, she rested her forehead against the cool glass, staring blankly at the heavy fall of night.

She was still in love with Hunter.

The simple knowledge emerged in her thoughts. It wasn't a new revelation. She'd always known she'd never be able to get over a love so deep in her heart. Over the years, she hadn't fallen out of love. She'd simply learned to bury it and carry on in a life without him.

Hunter, she knew, returned none of the same

feelings. Whatever he'd carried inside had been ripped away the day she'd told him it was over. It took only seconds for hardness to shadow his gray eyes while he shut down his heart. He didn't fight for her. He never again tried to contact her. He took what she said and went on with it.

She couldn't blame him. It had been her choice. The fact she'd washed away his love rested on her shoulders, no one else's.

What she needed was to quit thinking about things she couldn't change and concentrate on what she had some control over. Like getting as far away from him as possible.

A strong cup of coffee would clear her thoughts. Turning away from the window, she headed for the door and then gave the round knob a gentle twist. Peeking into the hallway, she saw Hunter propped up against the frame. His head rested on his shoulder as he slept uncomfortably in the chair.

As he slept—

Quietly, so she wouldn't wake him, she slipped back inside the room.

He was asleep, oblivious to what was happening around him. If there was ever a chance for her to get away, this was it. The coffee she originally had in mind was forgotten, leaving room for new ideas.

Slipping her feet into the tennis shoes she kept at the cabin, she inhaled a deep, calming breath. This wasn't going to be easy. Even if she did manage to get out of the cabin without him noticing, she still had a long, hard walk down the mountain. She didn't have a coat, and although it was summer, mountain nights were chilly.

She could do it though. This might be her only chance. It was now or never.

She cracked the door open, holding her breath. She waited for the hinges to creak or the floor to protest under her weight, but neither uttered a sound, leaving silence in the air.

In his chair, Hunter slept undisturbed. For a moment, she paused, taking one final look at his pure masculinity. Thick, dark eyelashes cast dark shadows against his rough cheeks. Large hands lay folded over his flat abdomen, and his broad chest rose and fell with each breath.

In another place, another time, she'd have given anything to stay and risk one more chance at the passion they'd shared. But, in this reality, there wasn't a chance of them staying together. For her protection, her own peace of mind, she had to get away. She had a life waiting for her back in Denver. One that didn't involve Hunter.

On the tips of her toes, she passed through the hall, half expecting to hear his deep voice explode behind her. At the end of the hallway, she turned back, making sure he was still asleep before rushing down the stairs with her heart beating wildly against her ribs.

"Goodbye, Hunter," she whispered into the still air before slipping out the front door, disappearing into the night.

****

Hunter waited until he heard the front door click into place before moving. She'd done exactly as he assumed when she stuck that pretty little head of hers out the door. Even with his eyes closed, he was aware of her every movement. He wasn't surprised when she tiptoed passed only a few minutes later.

Taking the stairs two at a time, he reached the front door in seconds. He didn't want to let her get too far ahead. He was only willing to play this little cat-and-mouse game of hers for so long before he dug his claws in, dragging the little mouse back to her hole.

He should just let the stubborn, irritating woman go. If she was dumb enough to try to make it off the mountain in the pitch of night, he should let her. He was tired of fighting to get her to believe him. Maybe he should let her go find her own answers, regardless of the risks.

The chilly breeze swept over him as he took his first step out the door. He caught her shadow ducking into a cluster of trees. Falling into line behind her, he was careful to keep his presence unknown. It wasn't an easy climb. The ground was rough with littered shrubs and scattered rocks. Other than the cabin, the rest of the mountain remained in its native state.

She moved fast on her feet, forcing him to pick up his pace to keep sight of her, ducking in and out of thick branches. Only the moon and the stars, glistening in the sky above, offered any sort of light to see by.

Damn woman. Didn't she know how foolish she was? Even if she didn't believe a word he'd told her about Grant, she at least had to realize how dangerous it was to be out here all alone. If she didn't fall and break her neck trying to handle the steep mountain slope, there was always the wildlife posing their own threat.

She stumbled, caught herself before landing on her rear end. He wondered if she realized she was leading them deeper and deeper into the cloak of the forest. Looking back, he could no longer see the cabin. He was swallowed in on all sides by thick groves of pine and aspen trees.

It was time to put an end to this before they wound up lost in the dark. Slicing his own path, he circled around the direction Paxton was headed. Out of the corner of his eye, he made sure her shadowed image was still visible as he worked his way in front of her. The woman actually thought she could do this when she wasn't even aware of his bulky form sneaking around.

He waited until she reached a clearing before stepping out from behind a tree. "Going somewhere?"

The scream that tore from her lips was loud enough to wake the dead. Wide, sapphire eyes flashed with fear. Even with the darkness, he could see her face turn white as chalk.

He'd scared her more than he thought he would.

Slowly, anger replaced the fear. Her eyes, only seconds ago cold with terror, heated quickly with rage. Pale skin turned into red fury as she formed fists at her sides.

"Damn you," she cursed through tight lips. "What in the world do you think you're doing, popping out at me like that? You scared me to death."

"Better me than some hungry mountain lion."

"Mountain lions don't eat people." Frustration built and left her wanting to land a fist in the center of his stomach.

"Maybe not. But they do tear them to pieces when someone trespasses on their turf." He watched her try to regain her composure. She pulled nervously at the hem of her shirt then yanked her fingers through her honey-blond hair. For a moment, he felt a stab of guilt for scaring her as her chest rose heavily with a deep breath.

"You're the only animal around here I'm afraid of." The fear disappearing, her voice settled back to calm. "I can't believe you scared me like that."

He took a step closer. "And I can't believe you tried to sneak away. Did you actually think you would have made it all the way to town?"

She lifted her chin. "Yes."

"Then I guess you're not as smart as I've given you credit for. What you pulled was a stupid stunt. One that could have gotten us hurt or even killed."

She took her own step in his direction, a mask of stony determination covering her face. "What I pulled was a desperate attempt to get away. You left me no other choice. I asked you to take me back, and you refused. Then you trashed the telephone. This was the only option I had left."

She didn't get it. He sucked in a hard breath, wanting to grab her, shake her until she saw reason. Lifting his hands, he dropped them over her slender shoulders. But instead of shaking her, he held her still under his harsh gaze.

"I'm warning you, princess, don't try something like this again. I won't be so forgiving the next time."

He had to give her credit when she didn't back down. With a look as harsh as his own, she stared at him without blinking an eye. "Don't threaten me, Hunter."

"That's not a threat. It's a promise."

For a moment, she stumbled, her tongue sneaking out of her mouth, running nervously along her bottom lip. His hold on her shoulders increased as he fought off the urges such a sight pushed through his body. Images of his own tongue tracing those lips, slowly tasting her sweetness as she surrendered to him, swarmed through his mind.

She straightened, bringing defiant eyes up to meet his. "I'm not afraid of you or anything you threaten to do to me."

She'd pushed him an inch too far, shattering what little control he had left. If she wanted to prove she wasn't afraid of him, then he'd let her do just that. Using the grip of his hands on her shoulders, he yanked her against him, her soft, pliant body slamming against his.

Her palms pressed against his chest as she struggled to get away. He refused to let go. Her sweet scent surrounded him while her closeness did unmentionable things to certain parts of his body. Only a saint could hold up under the temptation she posed, and he was far from anything saintly.

Lodging his finger under her chin, he brought her gaze up to his. "You're not afraid of me?"

She didn't answer, only shook her head.

"You should be." He lowered his mouth to hers and nipped at the bottom lip she'd licked only seconds before. It tasted as sweet and tantalizing as he knew it would.

She stiffened in his arms, but he held her face still with his hands as she tried to turn her head.

He refused to stop. What raged through his body had lain dormant for many years. His want for Paxton, his need for her, took over every sensible thought. Feelings of betrayal and passion, love and hatred, blended into one violent emotion.

In one swift move, he had her imprisoned against his aching need. A primal growl escaped as his lips captured hers in a kiss meant to both punish and please. She continued struggling for only a second more before melting into him and opening her mouth to his.

Her hands crept up his chest and over his shoulders to clasp at the nape of his neck. She pressed seductively against him, tipping her head back, which allowed him to deepen the kiss.

He took her surrender and swallowed it up. The taste of her on his lips surged through his loins. The feel of her soft, inviting curves against his rougher, harder lines taunted him.

He could lose himself in her depths. It would be so easy claiming her as his again.

But she wasn't his. She belonged to another man.

The chilling thought was equal to a splash of cold water poured over his heated skin. He grabbed her waist, lifting her away from him. The sudden distance between them made her stumble forward. Sapphire eyes, dark with desire, searched for an answer he couldn't give.

"We need to get back to the cabin." His voice was rough, agitated. "You go first. I'll follow."

Without a word, she did as he said. Turning her back on him, she retraced their steps through the trees. He fell into step behind her, keeping his eyes fastened straight ahead, ignoring the gentle sway of her back end.

****

They were halfway to the cabin before Paxton could think clearly again. She was so out of it, she hadn't even argued when Hunter ordered her back. Like an obliging wimp, she'd done exactly what he said, when what she should have done was insisted he either

63

take her into town himself or let her go on her own.

It was the kiss and her embarrassing reaction to it. She gave herself to him freely. He could have taken her right there on the hard, cold ground and she wouldn't have fought him.

Angry and frustrated, she stormed quickly through the thick trees. She wasn't a starry-eyed teenage girl anymore. She knew better than to give in to temptations better left alone. What kind of fool was she, letting one simple kiss completely take over?

It wasn't a simple kiss. It was much more than that. She didn't want to begin to think of everything that had passed between them when their lips met and their bodies melted together.

Ahead, the dark outline of the cabin came into view. She quickened her steps, eager to lock herself away. On the verge of breaking through the trees, Hunter's hand closed over her shoulder, pulling her back into the shadows.

"What are you doing?" She wrenched free from his hold. The last thing she needed was to be close to him again. Once had been enough.

"Shh." He pulled her deeper into the cloak of darkness.

"Let me go." She stuck her hands on her hips. "I just want to get inside and forget this night ever happened."

"The night isn't over yet. Look." He pointed a finger through the trees.

Following the direction of his finger, she caught the two dark forms hovering around. "Who's that?"

"My guess, they're Grant's friends."

Grant's friends.

This was it. This was her chance. He couldn't stop her when she had others backing her up. Spinning on her heels, she headed toward the cabin.

"Where do you think you're going?" He yanked her back.

"I'm going home." She shook free from his hold. "Since you refuse to take me, I'm sure those two will be more than happy to oblige."

"Oh, they'll be happy to oblige, but not with what you're thinking. Grant didn't send them to nicely take you back."

"And just what do you think he sent them for?" She stole another glance between the trees. They were still there, but they weren't trying to get inside. Instead, they moved around the outer walls, glanced in windows as they passed.

"They're here to find out what all you know about Grant. To make sure you don't talk like they made sure our informant didn't talk."

"I don't believe you." She turned away and started once again for the cabin. This time, she made it to the very edge of the trees before he stopped her.

"Look," he whispered in her ear. "Do you see what they're carrying?"

She did as he asked, her eyes straining in the dark to make shape of the objects they held in their hands. "Are those guns?"

She felt Hunter's nod against the side of her neck.

"Why would they be carrying guns up here?" She looked up at his profile etched in the shadows.

"Why do you think?" Even in the dark, she caught the flicker of impatience in his expression. "I told you, it wasn't a friendly call that brought them here."

Was he right? Were they here for something other than making sure she was okay?

She shook the absurd thought from her head. No. It was too outrageous to believe. There had to be another explanation why they were carrying guns. Maybe they were naïve city boys, afraid of the wildlife. She could certainly believe someone might feel safer against the threat of a bear or mountain lion if they had a gun in their hand.

"You still don't believe me, do you?"

"No." But her confidence wasn't as strong as it had been. There was something odd about the two. Not only were they armed, but they were stalking around like cats on the prowl for their prey. What good did it serve them wandering around outside, looking in windows the way they were?

They turned back toward the front of the cabin, giving her a better view. They were large men, intimidating faces carved from stone.

They didn't head for the front door as she'd expected. Instead they walked closer to the surrounding wilderness. Their voices grew more distinct as they approached the spot where she and Hunter crouched in the trees.

He pulled her into the cover of thick branches, but not far enough to where she couldn't hear what they were saying. Her ears perked up when their voices became clear. She held her breath while they drew closer.

"I don't see any signs of her." The shorter of the two stopped only feet away. "Maybe she's already left."

"Her car is still here." The taller one this time. "The license plate matches the name we were given."

"Then where is she? I don't plan on spending all night looking for this mystery woman who disappeared into thin air."

"You'll do what we were paid to do." The low growl of the voice sent a wave of shivers up Paxton's spine. "We find her, find out what she knows, then take care of her."

"Yeah, yeah. Easy money. I know."

She went numb from head to toe. The man's words echoed inside her head. They were looking for her…looking to take care of her. She wasn't dumb enough to believe that was meant in a good way.

Hunter had been right all along.

Grant, her wedding, her future, everything she believed in, was a lie. Everything she took to be true was anything but. Those men weren't sent to see her safely back to her loving fiancé. They were here to kill her, on Grant's orders. He wasn't worried about her wellbeing. He was worried about covering his own backside. If that meant taking out the woman he claimed to love, so be it.

The world began to spin. Her legs went weak. She swayed on her feet, vaguely aware of Hunter's strong arms wrapping around her, holding her tight to his side. Blackness threatened to take over, and she welcomed it. She needed to escape and get away from the horrible truth facing her.

"Paxton." Her name drifted from somewhere far away. She couldn't bring herself to acknowledge it.

"You can't give out on me now, princess. I need your help if we have any chance of getting out of here. Can you hold on long enough to get to the car?"

Though she didn't know how she did it, she

nodded. Some small part still fought the darkness. With unsteady steps, she allowed him to take her deeper into the trees. She questioned nothing. She knew if they were going to get out of this alive, she had to put her faith in Hunter.

Chapter Six

His senses had gone on alert long before the cabin came into sight. The inner voice inside his head shouted a warning too loud to be ignored. So it didn't surprise him to discover they were no longer alone on the mountain.

He knew the time was coming. It only ended up being sooner rather than later. Grant didn't waste time seeking his missing bride.

Against his side, Paxton slumped deeper into his hold, giving him the majority of her weight. He didn't have much time left before he lost her completely. Shock was taking over. It wouldn't be long before she gave in.

He'd wanted to prove he was telling the truth, but not like this. Overhearing those men talk about what they planned to do was a fate he never wanted her to face. She now had no choice but to believe what he said. But at what cost?

Patting the front pocket of his jeans, he was relieved to find the keys still safely tucked away inside. They had a way of escape. It was just finding the opportunity to do so. The Cherokee sat thirty feet out of reach. In their current situation, it was an awful long way to go.

The two uninvited guests changed their path. Turning toward the cabin, they started around the backside. Once they were out of sight, he knew he'd have to make a run for it and pray their luck was with them.

He inched closer to the clearing, keeping a steady eye on them. "We're going to make a run for it. Hold on tight, and I'll get us to the car."

Paxton gave an intangible sound in response. The best he could hope for at the moment. As long as she stayed on her own two feet, they'd be okay.

He unlatched the holster around his shoulder and pulled out his gun. Flicking off the safety, he rested his finger against the trigger. They hovered on the edge of the tree line with the Cherokee in their direct path. He watched, waited, muscles tense, body pumping with adrenaline.

They disappeared around the side of the cabin and he took the chance. Tightening the arm holding Paxton to his side, he pulled them out of cover, rushing toward the Cherokee. One eye remained focused on their destination while the other watched for their friends to return.

They reached the vehicle without notice. Pressing Paxton against the support of the passenger door, he dug the keys out of his pocket and unlocked the doors. Shoving her into her seat, he rushed around to the driver's side, careful not to slam doors. Once the engine fired up, their cover was blown. He didn't need to warn them beforehand.

He fumbled to hit the button for the ignition. Seconds from turning the engine over, their uninvited guests emerged. The automatic lights inside the Cherokee remained on, breaking through the darkness, calling out their presence.

In the same second, he brought the car to life as he pushed Paxton down further in her seat. "Hold on."

The two men ran as he threw the gear into reverse then planted his foot on the gas pedal.

Rocks spit under the tires as he backed down the drive. A bullet whizzed past the driver's side, too close for comfort. The next few seconds mattered more than anything. The men were making a mad dash for their car. It would only take a couple seconds before they were behind the wheel.

The first chance he got, he whipped the car around and threw it into drive. The sudden change tossed Paxton in her seat, but she remained silent, her eyes glazed over, face pale.

It was probably for the best. This wasn't an experience she needed to be part of.

Another bullet splintered the side window, but the glass stayed intact in its frame. Through the rearview mirror, he watched their car fighting to catch up. One hung out the window, aiming his gun while the other kept control of the car.

He pushed hard on the gas pedal, sending the speed to a dangerous limit on the curvy road. His knuckles turned white around the steering wheel as he sent up a silent prayer to get out of this alive.

His only chance of getting away was to test his skills against the other driver. Not only had he been given defensive driving courses during his training, he'd also spent his teenage years playing chicken down the mountain roads. A game he'd never lost.

"Let's play, fellows." With one hand on the wheel, he worked a seatbelt around Paxton's crumpled form and then did the same for himself.

He pushed the Cherokee faster. Behind him, the other car did the same.

The road curved dangerously up ahead, one side dropping off a high cliff into the rocks below. He released only a little pressure from the gas pedal, knowing he was going entirely too fast to make the turn.

He ignored the car trailing behind, forgot about the darkness of the night. His concentration rested on the road and the terrifying drop waiting for them if he made one wrong move.

He started into the turn with a heavy control over the steering wheel, keeping the tires in line with the curve of the road. As the twist grew deeper, the Cherokee fought harder to free itself. The speed and the wheels fought at opposite ends. It took everything he had to keep his steering steady.

The left side tires lost traction on the ground below, pushing into the air for a heart-stopping second before falling back with a hard thump. The jerk yanked the car in the other direction, pulling them toward the cliff. The steering wheel popped from his hands, spinning uncontrollably.

Releasing a string of curses, he grabbed the wheel. He had a window of only seconds to regain control before they toppled down the mountain. The muscles in his arms ached as he put every ounce of strength into turning the Cherokee away from the cliff, battling the force of nature with everything he had.

He heard the ground breaking away underneath the weight of the car. Adrenaline shot through with a brand new force. Finding a strength he didn't know he possessed, he wrenched the steering wheel back into a straight line seconds before the front tires slipped off the side.

They came out of the curve in a sloppy fishtail, but they were alive and that was all that mattered. Knowing time was of the essence, he slammed down on the gas pedal and sent them flying down the straight stretch of road. He stole a glance in his rearview mirror, watching the other car wrestle with the curve.

They skid out of the curve without harm, but before they had a chance to straighten out, the back of their car hitched against a huge rock jutting from the side of the road. The force of the hit sent them spinning around in the opposite direction, their taillights facing Hunter.

It was the break he needed. He took off, hoping it would take them awhile to get free. He worked his way down the remaining twists and turns, always with an eye on the rearview mirror.

Reaching town without any sight of them, he relaxed a touch. But he knew he wouldn't feel true relief until they were speeding down the interstate.

At this late hour, the roads were deserted. The town was shut down tight. He kept up his speed along the small highway, hoping there weren't any troopers hiding away in the shadows. Though his badge would be enough to get him out of a ticket, he couldn't afford the delay.

In her seat, Paxton mumbled. By the time they reached the interstate, color began to return to her face.

"You're okay." He dropped a gentle hand on her arm. "You can pull out of this. I know you can."

She didn't respond.

"Think good thoughts," he quoted old advice given

when he'd been knocked unconscious. "It will help pull you out of the darkness."

"Good thoughts," he repeated as he settled into the flow of traffic.

****

Hunter's voice sounded far away.

Paxton tried hard to concentrate, letting the familiar sound pull her from the numbness holding her captive. Slowly, she became aware of her surroundings, of the road speeding past and the warmth of his hand resting against her arm.

"Think good thoughts," he'd told her with a soft pat.

Good thoughts. She tried hard to dig for some. Pushing down past layers of memories, she grabbed onto one and let it drag her back to awareness.

"Good morning, princess," he greeted when she turned her head. "You missed all the excitement."

"We got away." It was more of a statement than a question. He was much too calm to still be running for their lives.

He nodded. "We did."

Still under the control of shock, she shivered in her seat, fighting off the hard pounding behind her temples. Her limbs were weak, exhausted. Her skin was cold to the touch.

"How are you doing?" He glanced at her beside him.

"I've been better." Her eyes traveled over him. "Why did you tell me to think good thoughts?"

He shrugged. "Years ago, I was knocked unconscious by a man who played baseball with my head. I blacked out. When I started coming back, a nurse was urging me out of the darkness by telling me to think good thoughts. It worked."

"It worked for me too."

He glanced at her, his gray eyes gentle. "I'm glad."

"Do you want to know what I thought of?" She knew she was avoiding the true topic needing to be discussed, but she wasn't up to that just yet. Finding out about her fiancé's lies and deception could wait.

Understanding her need to keep the conversation on safer ground, he nodded. "Tell me."

"It was my eighteenth birthday party at the country club. The night we first met."

Beside her, he stiffened but didn't stop her.

She rested back in her seat, closing her eyes, letting the memories take over. After the night she had, she deserved this one indulgence.

"You were such a rebel back then, carrying around a chip on your shoulder as big as the entire state of Colorado."

"Yeah…well. I was pretty bitter in those days."

"You were pretty handsome too." Behind closed lids, she saw him in a pair of faded blue jeans, an old worn T-shirt clinging to every muscle. He'd worked on the grounds of the country club, earning money to pay his way through college.

He'd come in during the middle of her party, planting himself at the bar and downing a beer in two, large gulps. He captured her attention from the moment he entered, holding on to it the rest of the night. "I remember coming up with some stupid excuse to talk to you."

"If I remember right, it had something to do with how I tended the flowers in the courtyard." He smiled at her. "You had some story about taking agriculture classes."

She groaned. "I knew it was stupid."

He laughed, and she opened her eyes. His eyes met hers, losing the guarded expression they usually carried. "Yeah, it was. But I didn't care. A beautiful girl wanted my attention. I wasn't about to call her on the lame line she chose to use."

"Oh, God, what you did to me back then." She sighed, forgetting about the tension, the anger, between them. For one stolen moment in time, there was no past between them. It was just her and Hunter. The way they used to be.

"I was enthralled. It was as if everyone else disappeared and only you and I remained."

That special softening, reserved for those on the verge of falling in love, swept through her. Tension drained away, leaving a small smile on her lips. "I can't believe I left my birthday party. I'd been looking forward to that night for months."

"Did you regret it?"

She shook her head. "No. I have never regretted that night. It was one of the best nights of my life."

"Mine too," Hunter admitted so quietly it was almost a whisper.

She watched him struggle with the memories she tossed between them. Under normal circumstances, she'd find herself in the same situation. But normal was something that had eluded her over the last couple days.

"There was dancing in the park, underneath the light of the stars." She floated back in time. "You took me to places I'd never been. That old Mexican restaurant serving the best green chili in town. The hilltop by the airport where we watched the planes land."

She could still hear the sound of rushing water from their stroll down the Platte River. He took her under the bridges where the homeless lived, showing her a side of life she'd never seen before. They followed the river through the lower streets of town where apartments crumbled into the streets and litter lined the sidewalks.

She hadn't been afraid or worried about her surroundings. She knew Hunter would keep her safe, protect her. In those areas, foreign to her until that night, he'd shown her a beauty she never knew existed. The bed of roses blooming on a windowsill. A man playing ball with his son under the streetlights.

"I was a sight in my pink, ruffled gown." She giggled like the teenager she'd been. "I stuck out like a sore thumb everywhere we went."

"Like a beautiful sore thumb," Hunter clarified.

"And when the night was over," she sighed. "You took me home and kissed me goodbye on the front porch."

Her body tingled with the playback of that kiss. So soft and tender it filled her heart with sweetness. She'd melted against him, flying on a cloud high above. He'd made her feel special, as if she was the only one who existed in his world.

Her eyes grew heavy as images from that first kiss flipped slowly through her mind. She turned to warm liquid inside while a deep calm blanketed her. There was no stress or tension left in her bones, only a soft glow of a love once cherished. A love unlike any she'd ever dreamt possible.

"I fell in love with you that night," she told Hunter in a sleepy voice before giving in to the dreams pushing at her. With a soft smile on her lips, she drifted asleep.

Chapter Seven

A gentle shake pulled her from sleep.

"Rise and shine."

Forcing her eyes open, she groaned when she saw the night lingered. It couldn't be time to get up yet. She still had at least a few hours left.

Curling into a ball, she closed her eyes.

"Paxton, you have to wake up long enough to get inside the room. I'm not carrying you."

The familiar rumble of Hunter's voice forced reality back. She wasn't at home, cuddled up in her nice, warm bed. She was in a terrible nightmare she couldn't wake from. One she'd yet to face completely.

With a long, tired stretch, she again opened her eyes and rolled her head, facing the driver's seat. "Where are we?"

"In a little town just outside Cheyenne."

She looked out the window, taking in the small, decrepit building they were parked in front of. Bare bulbs hung loosely from posts along each side of the building. A wave of night bugs zipped around the dingy light. What paint remained on the weathered wood was peeling away in chunks while the numbers lining the doors hung at odd angles.

"What is this place?"

"This wonderful place is the Buddy 'B' Motel." He smiled at her, enjoying the situation a little too much.

"Cheap Rates. Clean Rooms."

Dread welled inside. "Is this where we're staying?"

"Temporarily. Just long enough to get some sleep before we head out again."

She eyed the crumbling building and considered staying right where she was. She'd slept this long in the cramped space of the passenger seat. A few more hours wouldn't hurt.

Hunter cracked open his door, looking back before climbing out. "I know it's not the five star hotels you're used to, princess. But it's the best I can offer. Good old Grant wouldn't think to look for you in a place like this."

Grant. The mention of his name brought back the danger chasing her. Someone had come after her on his orders. Out there in the night, somewhere, two men looked for her with orders to take care of her.

Fear and shock threatened to take over again. Swallowing hard, she fought off the temptation to slip back into darkness. It wasn't going to do her any good. If she had any hope of a happy ending, she had to stay alert, aware.

She glanced at the motel. Hunter was right. Grant would never think to look for her in a place like this. She doubted he was even aware such places existed. If they didn't carry limousine service and penthouse suites, he knew nothing about them.

"Well…are you daring enough to enter?"

Daring enough…no. Frightened enough…yes.

She climbed out and met Hunter at the front fender. He flashed a key in his palm, unlocking the door with a rusted number five dangling in the center. "I let you sleep while I registered us at the front desk." He stepped back, letting her enter ahead of him. "A place like this didn't much care who was with me as long as I was willing to pay the price."

The mention of money brought a stark reality. For the first time in her life, she was stranded without a penny to her name. Everything—her cash, her checkbook, her credit cards—was left back in the dressing room at the church. She didn't even have identification proving who she was.

The roles were reversed between her and Hunter. He was the one holding the money while she had nothing. Financially, she had to depend on him completely. The thought wasn't comforting. It had taken her a long time to break free of her father's financial hold. The idea of hovering close to the same with Hunter left her uneasy.

"Welcome to your castle, princess." He swept his hand around the tiny, cramped room.

Centered on a dark orange carpet sat a double bed with a faded comforter of questionable colors covering a dipping mattress. Across from the bed, a dresser was pushed against the wall, an eighties-style television resting on its pockmarked surface.

"At least it's clean." With the view from outside, she was afraid of the filth hiding behind closed doors. Though it was rundown and furnished with outdated pieces, there wasn't a speck of dust to be found.

"It's only for tonight," Hunter reassured her.

What there was left of it. Paxton wondered what time it was. It hadn't been that late when she'd tried sneaking away from the cabin. But she had no idea how many hours had passed since part of the night remained a blur.

She thought of her refusal to believe a word Hunter told her and the accusations she'd slung his way. No matter how much she'd refused to believe him, he'd been right all along.

If it weren't for him, she'd be married to Grant, naive to his true self. How long would she have floated in the dark, knowing nothing of his sinister side? And if she had found out, somewhere through their marriage, where would that have left her?

Dead.

The single word echoed inside her head. She shivered as she thought of what her life would have become if she'd married Grant. Hunter had not only saved her from some unwanted questioning when he kidnapped her, he also may have saved her life.

Without thinking about what she was doing, she pushed onto her toes, planting a soft kiss on his rough cheek. "Thank you."

His eyes widened in surprise. "For what?"

"For making sure I didn't marry a man like Grant. Who knows where I would have ended up if I had."

"Don't thank me, yet. My little stunt put your life in danger. Save the gratitude until I get us both out of this alive."

She sat down on the edge of the bed, the worn springs sagging under her weight. Clasping her hands in her lap, she stared down at her entwined fingers. "I need to know about him, Hunter. I need to know what he's into."

She glanced up and met his probing gray gaze. "I have so many questions. I can't understand how I didn't know what kind of man my fiancé was. I never thought I was a fool. But I guess if the shoe fits—"

The mattress beside her sagged as he sat next to her. "Grant has many people fooled, not just you. Heck, even the Bureau can't get a good lead on him. He's good at what he does and even better at covering his tracks."

"What exactly is it that he does? What is he doing that he's willing to kill people to keep it secret?"

Hunter pushed up from the bed so he stood directly in front of her. "Tomorrow I'll answer all your questions, I promise. Tonight, we both need to get some sleep."

She knew he was right, but she doubted she'd be able to get much more sleep. With a rational mind once again, her head buzzed with what ifs and whys.

He moved behind her and grabbed a pillow off the bed. "I'll take the floor. You take the bed."

She glanced down at the orange carpet. Aged and wearing away in many places, it didn't look comfortable. She thought of the last two nights he'd spent sleeping in a chair outside her door. She couldn't make him suffer any longer.

"Hunter," her voice was low when she spoke.

Dropping the pillow on the floor, he looked up. "What?"

"The bed is big enough for the two of us."

"I don't think that would be a good idea." When his eyes met hers, she knew he remembered the kiss back on the mountain. "I think we're both better off if I sleep on the floor tonight."

"We're grown adults with reasonable control over our hormones. I don't think one night in the same bed is going to hurt us. You and I both know what happened back at the cabin was a mistake. And neither of us have a desire to repeat such a mistake."

He looked at her for a long stretch without saying a word. She waited patiently. With a shrug, he bent down, grabbed the pillow from the floor, and tossed it back on the bed.

She took the gesture as his agreement, which was exactly what she wanted. Wasn't it?

Her heart paused for a beat when he pulled his shirt up over his head, tangling his ebony hair as he did. Dark skin flexed tightly over his chest. A light dusting of black hair guided a path down to his waist, disappearing beneath the top of his jeans. He was firm, hard, and one hundred percent male.

His husky scent tickled her nose while her eyes caressed the long stretch of his body. Maybe this wasn't such a good idea after all. Those hormones she claimed she could handle were kicking to life and she was having a hard time settling them down.

To distract herself, she made a show of bending down to unlace her shoes, kicking them into a pile on the floor. This was crazy, getting so worked up over the sight of Hunter naked from the waist up. It wasn't like this was the first time she'd seen him this way.

She was a grown woman, an adult, she could handle the sight of a half-naked man. With a wave of determination, she ventured back up from the floor and helped Hunter pull the comforter down over the mattress. Even with her resolve, she was careful to keep her eyes trained on the motions of her hands rather than on the man standing on the other side of the bed.

"You go ahead and crawl into bed," he told her when the crisp white sheets underneath the blankets greeted them. "I want to make sure we're locked in tight before I turn in."

Glancing up from the bed, her eyes clashed with his, sucking the air from her lungs. Unable to form a word, she could only nod. Their gazes locked for what felt like an eternity before he finally turned away and strolled over to the door to slap the dead bolt into place.

I can do this. Repeating the chant, she eased under the sheets, careful to stay close to her side of the bed. She heard his shuffled steps as he moved through the tiny room. Felt the dip of the mattress as he settled his long, hard body next to hers.

All she had to do was roll over and go to sleep. Once dreams came, she'd no longer be aware of him in bed next to her. With her back to him, she curled into a ball and forced her eyelids shut, willing sleep to come.

****

She may have been fine sharing a bed but it was killing him. Stretched stiff as a board on the flimsy mattress, Hunter was achingly aware of Paxton curled beside him. Her gentle scent washed over him as her soft breath echoed in his ears.

What had he been thinking? He should have known his body would instantly overreact to being so close to her soft, enticing curves. He wasn't made of steel, and it had been an awfully long time since he'd had a woman in his bed.

Any other woman, though, wouldn't have caused the same reaction. She'd been the only one holding such a power over him, able to make him forget about everything except her.

It certainly didn't help she'd yanked them back to that first night they'd spent together. A night he'd shoved deep in his vault of unwanted memories. He'd been the one to tell her to think good thoughts. But how could he have known what she would return with?

Beside him, she stirred, stretching her long legs out. Although they were hidden underneath the covers, they captured his memory of another time when those legs had been trapped underneath the blankets with him. Only then, they'd been wrapped tight around his body and tangled with his own.

Swallowing a groan, he tossed his arm over his eyes, hoping to block out the delectable sight. He couldn't soften toward her. It would only prove to be his downfall.

He had a job to do. He needed to concentrate on keeping her safe until Grant's arrest. The woman lying beside him was still the same Paxton who'd driven a stake through his heart ten years ago. He'd be doing himself a favor to remember that.

She'd never looked back that day she'd confessed he was nothing more than a summertime fling, a way to pass the months before she started at the University. It was the same day he'd planned to ask her to marry him. The small engagement ring, costing him more than two months' rent on his tiny apartment, had been hidden away in his pocket.

He wasn't sure what had taken a worse toll on him, the pain or the embarrassment. Both emotions roared through as he watched her walk away. It was the last time he ever trusted his heart to a woman. The last time he let anyone get close enough to care about them.

Bitterness welled inside, and he grabbed on to it. He had to hold tight to that bitterness and remember what she'd done to him. It was the only way to get away from her unharmed.

Chapter Eight

His internal alarm clock roused Hunter after only a few hours of sleep. A thin strip of sunlight broke through the dark brown curtains draped over the window. It was faded light, hinting at the early hours of dawn.

The blankets, tossed carelessly over his legs, tightened as Paxton, still asleep, turned from her back to her side.

It was a surprise he'd gotten any sleep. How long had he lain awake, willing himself to block out her presence at his side? Even the bitterness he reclaimed did little to keep away the temptation of the beautiful woman beside him. At least it kept him from reaching out, cuddling her against his side. He'd been a good little boy, keeping his hands to himself the entire time.

Careful not to disturb her, he slid off the side of the bed. It wouldn't hurt anything to give her another hour or two of sleep. He would have taken it himself if he thought he'd actually drift back. But now that he was up, he knew it was for good.

He kept his feet light, heading for the bathroom at the back of the room. At the edge of the bed, he stopped, captured by the peace falling over Paxton as she slept.

He knew it was a short-lived peace. Sleep kept her brain from working over what had happened. When she woke up the truth would still be there, and whatever escape she might have been able to find would be gone.

He had to give her credit. When things looked bleak last night, she'd held on long enough for them to get away. It was more than he would have expected from someone who just learned their fiancé hired someone to kill them.

And even after her shock passed, she didn't linger in its depths. She'd asked for answers. Answers he'd give later today.

She was a strong woman, but he'd always known that. She may have grown up underneath her father's overprotective wing, but that hadn't stopped her from building a strength she could depend on.

With one last lingering look, a treat he told himself he deserved, he closed himself inside the bathroom.

If he thought the main room was small, the bathroom was something else entirely. It went past small, past cramped. Somehow, they'd fit a sink, tub and toilet into a space no bigger than a broom closet. Standing in the center of the cracked linoleum floor, he was less than an arm's length away from each.

When he looked above the tub, the showerhead, hanging dangerously off the end of a copper pipe pushed through the wall, looked ready to fall off. A quick scan of the space between the tub and shower showed nowhere near enough room for his over six-foot height.

Hell. He desperately needed a shower. Too many days had passed without one. Soon he wouldn't have any problem keeping Paxton away, his scent alone would do it.

He started the water before stripping out of his

jeans and briefs. He had to bend his knees, pull his head all the way back in order to fit, but ten uncomfortable minutes later he was clean.

It took another five minutes to dress and hand-comb his hair. When he stepped out of the bathroom, Paxton had yet to wake up. Grabbing his gun and phone, he slipped outside. Hooking the holster over his shoulder, he punched in the familiar number.

Staying by the door, he leaned against the wooden structure and waited for his call to be answered.

"Smith," his partners voice barked over the line.

Hunter grimaced, wondering what caused the frustration coming through. "Bad morning?"

"Reeves. It's about time you called. Williams is having a fit, waiting to hear from you."

"What's his problem?" Though he could already guess, he hoped the answer was different than what he expected.

"He wants you to stand down." Smith's tone lowered, confirming what he didn't want to hear. "He's not convinced Paxton needs to be placed under protective custody."

"They came after us last night. Two of them."

"Grant's men?" Interest peaked in his partner's voice.

"That's what I'm figuring." He pushed away from the wall. There was no way he was going to allow Williams to take him away from Paxton. He'd quit the Bureau before he let that happen.

"Maybe this will change things."

"Doesn't matter if it does. I'm Paxton's shadow until Grant is arrested."

"Maybe she can help get her fiancé behind bars

quicker than we can."

Coming to a stop in front of the Cherokee, Hunter hitched a foot against the front bumper. "She doesn't know anything about his doings. I'm sure of it."

"Maybe not. But she knows people close to him who might be part of his operation. Ask her about The Watcher. Maybe she'll have some names for us."

He didn't see any harm in it. Smith could be right. She just might give them the lead they needed. "I'll ask."

They wrapped up their conversation quickly after that. When he stepped back into the room, Paxton was sitting up in bed, blankets pulled to her hips. Honey-blond hair fell in a messy wave of curls around her face. Sapphire eyes still held the look of sleep.

Lifting her arms above her head, she clasped her fingers together in a long stretch, and gave him a weak smile. "I was wondering where you were."

He tried ignoring the hem of her shirt lifting with her raised arms, exposing a flash of creamy skin. "I had a call to make. I took it outside so I wouldn't disturb you."

"I don't suppose you can tell me they've arrested Grant and we can go home."

Oh, how he wished he could. With the ideas running through his head at the moment, he'd give anything to be able to take her home. Instead, all he could do was shake his head.

"Sorry. No such news. Right now, we don't have anything solid to hold him on even if we take him in."

She dropped her arms, and he heaved a sigh of relief. "So what do we do now?"

"Now, we move on." He looked over her shoulder,

needing to see something—anything—besides the temptation she presented. "I know a place where we'll be safe."

She rose from the bed. "Where?"

"It's a place I know. Trust me, Grant won't find you there."

She circled around the bed and came to a stop a few feet away. "Look, Hunter, I know you're the professional here, but it's my life we're dealing with. At least give me the courtesy of telling me where we're headed."

She was right. She had every right to know what was going on. Somewhere down the line, her life might depend on it.

"A buddy of mine has a hunting cabin outside of Yellowstone. It's always been mine to use whenever I feel the need."

"And now you feel the need," she finished for him.

He nodded.

"Do I have time to take a shower?"

"We're in no rush. More than likely, Grant is regrouping after last night. For the time being, we're relatively safe."

In her eyes, he saw her desperate need to believe him. Sheltered for her whole life, this little adventure had to be taking its toll. Where he was used to living on the edge, never knowing what the next day might bring, she knew nothing of that kind of life. Her days were carefully planned out on a daily calendar so there was never a question of what tomorrow might bring.

Before he realized what he was doing, he reached for her, curling his hands over her small shoulders, giving a tight squeeze. "I'm going to take care of you," he promised without a trace of doubt in his voice. "We're in this together."

Her teeth nibbled on her bottom lip in worry, but she nodded.

He turned her toward the bathroom. "Go. Take a shower." He gave her a small shove in the right direction. "And then we'll get out of here."

She slipped from his hold, closing herself away in the bathroom. A few minutes later, the sound of running water filled the room. For a moment, he didn't move as his imagination got the better of him.

He pictured her standing naked underneath the shower, water dripping down her bare skin, flowing over her luscious body. He hardened as he thought of her honey-blond hair long and wet, flowing behind her as she lifted her face to the spray.

It took every ounce of resistance not to barge into the bathroom and join her. He hummed an unknown tune inside his head as he moved through the room, hoping to drown out the sounds of temptation. The harder his resistance was tested, the louder his humming became until it boomed inside the four walls.

His pacing brought him up short at the bed he and Paxton had shared. Desperate to keep his mind off the woman standing naked underneath the shower, he pulled the sheets and blankets over the mattress. While he worked, he hummed, louder and louder. The frantic pace of his tune matched the swift race of his hands sweeping over the bed.

"Hunter."

The sound of his name, almost a yell, brought his tune to a quick halt. Turning away from the bed, he found Paxton watching him. Damp curls fluttered around her tender face, stroking her cheeks.

"I…umm…think they have maids to do that." Her gaze fell to the newly made bed then returned to where he stood.

He stepped away from the bed. "Yeah, I guess you're right." He ran a hand through his hair and pulled in a ragged breath, thankful her shower was done and over with.

She glided across the room to settle on the corner of the bed, teasing him with the delicate curve of her back as she bent down to put her shoes on. Damp curls tumbled down and his hands itched to run through them, to feel the softness wrap around his fingers while the strands passed through his touch.

With a silent curse, he ground his hands into tight fists behind his back. He summoned up the bitterness he found the night before and latched on to it. "We should be going."

Straightening, she nodded. Falling into step behind him, she followed him out the door.

"After I drop the key off, we'll find a store where we can pick up a few essentials," he told her from behind the steering wheel.

"Good," she breathed in relief. "I was beginning to wonder how long I'd have to walk around with the same set of clothes on my back."

It only took a second to move them from their room to the front office. "Lock the doors," he ordered on his way out. "I'll be back in a minute."

As he walked away, he heard the click of the locks, and was happy she'd followed his orders. Inside the tiny office, a young boy, no more than eighteen, greeted him with an arrogant smile.

"Here to check out?" He held his hand out for the key.

Hunter dropped it in his palm as he eyed the baseball cap on top of his head. Still looking new, it sported the logo of a national football team. "How much for the hat?" He dug into his back pocket, pulling out his wallet.

"You want my hat?" The teenager reached up and touched the brim. "Why?"

"Let's just say I like it." Unfolding his wallet, he pulled out a twenty, hoping that would cover it.

The boy looked down at the twenty, back at Hunter. "You know you can get these just about anywhere."

"I don't have the time to shop around."

"All right." With a shrug, he pulled the hat off his head. Tossing it on the counter, he grabbed the twenty. "It's not like I don't have a dozen more at home."

"Thanks." Hunter hooked the rim of the hat with his finger as he left the office.

Nearing the Cherokee, he heard the click of locks disengaging. *Good girl.* She was paying attention to what happened around her.

"Do you have a pair of sunglasses?" He crawled into the driver's seat.

She opened the glove box, withdrew a pair of dark tinted sunglasses with red frames.

"Here." He tossed the hat at her. "With this and those, your appearance should be well hidden."

"Do you think that's necessary?" She palmed the hat, examining the stitching on the front. "I hardly doubt anyone out here is going to know who I am."

"You're probably right. But I don't want to take

any chances."

Carefully guiding them into traffic, he headed for Cheyenne. In Wyoming, where the towns were few and far between, he figured the capital city was their best bet in finding a discount store.

"Don't hide away all your hair," he instructed. "We don't want it to look like you're trying to hide under there. Just make sure the brim is pulled low over your face."

She nodded. Planting the hat on her head, she pulled her honey-blond hair into a ponytail through the back of the hat. Sticking the glasses on the bridge of her nose, she turned to him. "How do I look? Think I'm safe to walk the public streets?"

He spared her a glance. She'd done well in pulling the brim down, shadowing her prominent features. But her beauty still shined through. Though she wouldn't be recognizable on first look, he knew much more than that would give her away. There was something about her, her brilliance, that made it impossible for her to hide.

"I suppose you'll do." He smiled before turning back to the road.

They rode in silence the rest of the way. Reaching Cheyenne, it didn't take long to find what he was looking for. Pulling to a stop in the crowded parking lot of a popular discount store, he cut the engine and turned to Paxton.

"We get in and get out. I don't think we're in danger, but the less time we're out and about, the better."

She nodded and gave a final tug on the baseball cap, pulling the brim lower. Side by side, they entered the store. He grabbed a basket at the doors and led the way through the aisles.

It wasn't long before he realized even the simple task of shopping with Paxton was enough to create a fever inside. It took seconds to grab a pack of white briefs, toss them into the basket. A pack of socks, some clothes, and he was done.

Paxton on the other hand, took more time. Her clothes went smoothly enough, T-shirts and shorts to cover the basics. It was the undergarments causing him pain. Try as he might, he couldn't ignore her fingers as they passed over the silky selections. She grabbed a color assortment of panties holding hardly any material then found the bras to match.

It was going to be hell over the next few days. Every time he saw her he'd wonder which colors she had on underneath, his fingers itching for the chance to find out. To make matters worse, she filled the basket with honeysuckle scented body lotion and a light wildflower scented perfume.

Great, when he wasn't thinking about what she was wearing, he'd wonder which aroma she'd chosen to cover her body with. Would it be wildflowers or honeysuckle? Would she be wearing the red lace or the blue silk?

He'd been given his fair share of hard cases. But being close to Paxton without getting too close was going to be the hardest case he'd ever faced.

****

Paxton couldn't figure out what ran through Hunter's head. He looked angry when she picked up a small bottle of perfume. Maybe he thought she was wasting money buying such frivolous things. Maybe the dollar signs were adding up inside his head, and he wasn't happy with the totals he was getting.

"I promise, as soon as I'm home, I'll pay you back." She pulled her items out of the basket. In piles, she tossed her clothing onto the black belt moving slowly toward a bright-eyed cashier.

Hunter followed her. "Don't worry about it. The Bureau pays all expenses so consider this a gift from your government."

He stepped up to the cashier, pulling his wallet out of his back pocket. The woman, no more than twenty-one, smiled brightly, green eyes twinkling.

"How are you this morning?" she asked sweetly, taking absolutely no notice of Paxton stepping up at Hunter's side.

"I'm good." He offered a smile that the other woman swallowed up.

She passed one of his shirts over the scanner. "I bet green is a good color on you, what with your dark skin and all."

"In that case, I'll be sure to wear that one first."

Paxton almost gagged. The cashier was flirting, and he had no problem giving it back. Neither of them seemed to notice her standing there.

The cashier fluttered her eyelashes, smiled, a light, feathery lift to her lips that Paxton recognized immediately. The little snot was being coy, acting cute in front of the big, handsome man. It was an old act. There was no way he would fall for it.

She glanced at Hunter, waiting for him to clench his mouth in that tight line of his. That's what he'd do if she tried smiling at him like that.

Her mouth dropped open, and she came close to

sputtering in protest, when he returned the smile with one of his own.

"Cash or charge?" The cashier asked in a hushed, sultry voice.

Paxton had to clamp her hands behind her. She was tempted to choke that darn voice down where it belonged. It was a bedroom voice. And the last time she'd checked, they weren't in any kind of bedroom.

"Cash." Hunter held out a hundred-dollar bill.

Long, red painted nails grazed his skin as she took the money. Paxton was sure she was going to be sick.

"Have a nice day." The cashier handed back his change and waved with a trickle of fingers.

"You too." Hunter shot her one last smile before collecting the bags and stepping away for the next customer.

Paxton seethed as they made their way outside. As soon as the bright sunlight warmed her arms, she turned on him. "I can't believe you."

"What?" His gray eyes widened.

"You know what. You were flirting with that woman."

He opened the back hatch of the Cherokee, tossing the bags in one by one.

"I wasn't flirting. I was just being nice."

"You were being sickening," she countered. "Both of you were. It was embarrassing standing there, watching it."

"Don't you think you're exaggerating? She was a friendly woman, that's all."

She waited until they slammed their doors before going on. "If she was so friendly, why is it she didn't have a single word to say to me?"

Slinging an arm along the back of her seat, his eyes grazed over her. "You sure are making a big deal out of nothing. If I didn't know better, I'd say you were jealous."

"Jealous," she repeated. "I hardly think so."

He inched forward until his lips were only a couple inches from hers. "I was only being friendly. If you want to see flirting, I can show you flirting."

Her breath caught in her throat, and her heart pounded against her chest. He was so close she could see the lines etching his face. His musky scent surrounded her.

Reaching out, he hooked a finger under her chin, tilting her face up to his. "Trust me, princess, whatever you saw in there was nothing compared to what I'm capable of."

Images of a younger Hunter's seduction, with nothing more than words, exploded inside her head. She knew what he was capable of. His capability had brought her to her knees more than once.

She opened her mouth to speak but clamped it shut when his gray eyes darkened into a thunderous sky. His finger slipped from her chin to caress her cheek.

"That woman," he breathed. "Was just an innocent having some fun."

His lips brushed lightly against hers. "You, on the other hand, are far from being innocent. You know where that fun can lead."

She barely found the strength to nod. The breathing air inside the Cherokee seemed to disappear, replaced by a fierce heat burning up her neck. He captured the sides of her face in his large hands and held her steady as his lips found hers.

Her pulse froze as he nibbled a path along her bottom lip. He tempted with the promise of his kiss, never fully taking her mouth, teasing until she couldn't stand another second.

When he finally took her, she whimpered in relief, falling into him, surrendering. There was no denying she wanted this. *Oh how she wanted this.* It felt so right, so complete. His lips melted with hers and their hearts beat to the same tune as their passions flared.

She wanted more, so much more, but before she grasped what was happening, he broke away. Her head spinning, she tried breaking through the fog holding her captive.

"That, princess, is how I flirt."

Without another word, leaving her to wonder where she'd lost control, he kicked the Cherokee to life and backed away from the parking spot.

It was a good ten miles later, along with a long session of silent scolding, before she was able to push the kiss from her mind and face Hunter without blushing.

He'd played a game, punishing her for accusing him of flirting. And she'd been his easy pawn.

Turning to look out the side window, she squared her shoulders in renewed strength. She'd slipped, but she could guarantee herself, and Hunter, there wouldn't be a rematch.

Chapter Nine

The journey to the cabin swallowed up what was left of the day. Night settled by the time Hunter stopped in front of a small log cabin tucked tight in the mountainside. In comparison to the last cabin, this one came out looking the equal of a dollhouse.

It was welcoming, though, and comfortable. Handmade quilts draped the back of a chair and stretched out along the couch. A large redbrick fireplace provided heat.

Standing in the center of the main room, Paxton was happy they were here. It was a hundred times better than the motel room they'd left behind.

And it was far away from Grant.

"I'll start a fire." Hunter dumped their purchases on the couch. "Why don't you see what's stocked in the cupboards for dinner. After we eat, we'll talk."

The supplies were limited, but she was able to find a couple cans of chili. A seasoning rack above the stove offered enough spice to add some flavor.

By the time he hauled in a load of firewood and started the fire, she had dinner waiting on the table. The only drinks she could find were cans of root beer. Selecting two, she poured them into glasses and set them next to their bowls.

"There wasn't an awful lot to choose from." She joined him at the table.

Picking up his spoon, he shoveled in the first bite, and nodded in approval. "Tomorrow we'll go into town and pick up enough groceries to get us through a few days."

"How long do you think we'll have to stay?" She took a bite of her own chili.

He shrugged. "Hopefully, we'll be safe here until things with Grant are settled. But I don't know how long that'll take."

It was almost too much to grasp. She was surrounded by a nightmare she couldn't wake up from. A week ago, her life was normal. She was preparing for her wedding while packing up her house to put it on the market. She had her job, friends, and a life she considered comfortable.

And here she was, just a short time later, running from the man who'd claimed to love her. She couldn't talk to anybody. Couldn't even make a decision on her own. Everything depended on cornering Grant. Her safety. Her freedom. Her return to everything she knew. It all relied on finding something to put him behind bars where he belonged.

"If the FBI knows about him, why can't they just arrest him?"

"Believe me, we wish it was that easy." Hunter shook his head, obviously frustrated. "But Grant is good at keeping his hands clean, away from his dirty work."

She pushed her bowl away, suddenly losing her appetite. Food didn't seem to matter so much anymore. Only getting to the truth mattered. She had to know everything there was to know about Grant. Everything she'd been blind to.

"The Grant I knew, the one I agreed to marry, was a dedicated businessman. Robinson Enterprises is a well-respected company across the country. He inherited the business from his father, who inherited it from his father."

"There are no illegal claims against Robinson Enterprises. But we do believe he uses his company as a cover for his other dealings."

"Like what?" Unable to sit a second longer, she pushed away from the table. Gathering his empty bowl with hers, she put her restless energy into washing the dishes. Keeping her hands busy helped ease her nerves.

"The Bureau has a long list." He remained in his seat, watching her. "Though we can't prove it in a court of law, we've got him pinned down for everything from drug smuggling, to money laundering, to murder."

"Murder." The word stuck like a thorn in her throat.

She thought of the men who'd come after her, the informant and agents Hunter told her about. She'd shared the same bed, almost the rest of her life, with a man who placed no importance on human life. A man who did away with anyone who proved to be a problem.

"I don't understand." She turned back to Hunter. Her hands curled around the counter at her back, holding up her weight. "How can he be a part of all that and get away with it?"

"He's slick. One of the best I've seen. He knows enough to keep his prints off anything illegal. Whatever he wants done, he has another man in charge take care of it so he stays safely in the background."

"So he sits untouched while others take the fall."

He nodded. "The informant we had in custody was willing to sell him out in order to save himself. But most won't take that risk. They'd rather sit the rest of their lives in jail than face what Grant might do to them if they talk."

"So who's this other man he hides behind?"

"We don't know. On the streets, he goes by the nickname, *The Watcher*. But no one knows his actual name."

Pushing up from his chair, he joined her at the counter. "Whoever this Watcher is, he has to be someone close to Grant. Someone who is with him at all times. He'd have to know every detail of the operation and would have Grant's complete trust."

"Surely the FBI would be able to figure out who that might be."

"We've tried. But Grant is so elusive we've had a hard time keeping our fingers on what he's doing or who he's with."

He stepped up, tugged on her hands. Freeing them from the counter, he collected them in his own. "You could help us. You might be the one who knows who this Watcher is."

"How would I know? I never even knew what Grant was up to."

"That's exactly why you might know. Grant knew you were naive about him. He may have let his defenses down around you."

She shook her head, not entirely convinced. If the FBI couldn't get a lead on this person they called *The Watcher*, how was she supposed to know who he was?

Even as denial ran through her mind, an image flashed before her eyes, so fresh and clear, it left her wondering. The image wasn't of Grant but another man.

"There might be someone," she stated softly, unsure of her words.

He tightened his hands around her. "Don't doubt yourself. There's no punishment if you're wrong."

Except maybe having to live the rest of my life on the run.

"His name is Tony Bulto. He's Grant's chauffeur and his unofficial butler."

Inside her mind, she replayed how many times she'd heard Grant speak of Tony. The different things he handled for him. Though he kept a low profile when Grant ventured out in public, he was never far away when needed.

"Tony Bulto," Hunter repeated. "Is there anyone else?"

She shook her head. "I'm sorry. He's the only one who comes to mind."

"That's all right." He released her hands to yank his telephone from his waist. "You did great. Who knows, maybe we'll get lucky this time and find what we're looking for."

He turned his attention to the call, barely noticing when she slipped away. Inside, she was a mess, facts and reality weighing heavy on her shoulders.

A cold darkness threatened to settle. She knew she couldn't give in to it again. Weakness wasn't a trait she chose to carry. It was through strength she'd survived her mother's death when she was a child as well as her break-up with Hunter so long ago.

Relying on herself, her strength, was her only salvation in some of the worst times of her life. It had never escaped her before. She wasn't about to let it get away now when she needed it most.

Hunter would protect her the best he could. But she knew her own safety rode on her shoulders. She had to be alert, aware of what was happening around her. She had to remain focused on staying alive, on beating Grant and earning back her freedom. There were no other options.

Fighting off the threat of shock, she busied herself with the bags tossed on the couch. The logs behind her cracked and cackled as she separated her things from Hunter's, creating neat piles along the back of the couch.

****

Smith had been eager for the name. Though they knew not to get their hopes up, they had another lead. And in Grant's case, they came few and far between.

His conversation over, Hunter found Paxton working full force on the bags. Though she worked with resolve, she carried a faraway look, putting her thousands of miles away from the tiny cabin.

He wondered if she thought of Grant. Was it killing her knowing the man she loved was nothing like she'd imagined? Did she still love him? Was her heart still in his hands, even after learning what kind of man he was?

He wasn't sure he wanted the answers. Thinking of Paxton with another man tore at his gut. He had no right to her, but there was still part of him that continued to see her as his own.

"Here, let me help." He gathered a pile into his arms, left her alone in the room as he stowed them away before returning for more.

Once he'd cleared the couch, Paxton settled in the

corner closest to the fire, staring into the crimson red flames.

"Do you want to talk about it?" He settled in the opposite corner.

His voice startled her, dragging her attention away from the fire. She flashed a weak smile that never reached her sapphire eyes.

"Everything is so jumbled inside my head. I can't begin to put it into words." She shook her head and sighed. "It's not every day someone finds out the man they were going to marry is a hardened criminal."

Hunter moved closer. Her need, her pain, called to him. Old protective instincts sparked to life. It was what had gotten him into this mess in the first place and was now proving to do the same all over again.

She turned back to the fire. "I really thought I knew him. There were times I questioned some of the things he did, but I never imagined him to be the kind of man you say he is."

She turned away from the fire, her eyes focusing on him. When Hunter opened his mouth to talk, she held up her hand to stop him. "There's nothing you can say to make this easier, and I'm not about to sit around in self-pity."

He gathered her trembling hands into his and folded them in his warmth. "I wouldn't expect you to."

"I just can't stop the memories running through my head. I keep thinking of the business trips Grant was always taking. The privacy he insisted on every time his phone rang."

Her expression was so vulnerable, he ached to wipe it away. "I didn't think much of it. But now, every move he made seems suspicious. I keep wondering how many times I was around when he conspired someone's murder or sent someone to sell drugs to a teenage kid."

"I might be as guilty as him." She dropped her gaze. "He liked to vacation in exotic countries. Who knows what I was unaware of while we were there. I could have done things to help him without ever knowing."

He pulled on her hands, bringing her eyes back to his. "You're no more guilty than I am. All the blame falls squarely on his shoulders."

"But what if—"

He silenced her with a finger to her lips. "Don't tear yourself apart," he ordered in a gentle tone. "It won't do any good."

She nodded. "I know."

Her chest lifted with a heavy sigh. He knew it wasn't easy letting go. Guilt reflected in the blue depths of her eyes. A guilt she had no reason to feel.

He tucked a stray strand of hair behind her ear and let his fingers trail down, gently caressing her jawline. She was exhausted, mentally and physically. He wanted nothing more than to wrap her in his arms and kiss away her pain until he was the only thought on her mind.

Instead, he rose from the couch, pulling her with him. Her hands clasped in his, he urged her close. "Go to bed. Rest will do you some good."

"But what about you? I can't make you sleep on the floor."

He swept his knuckles over her pale cheek. "The couch folds out into a bed. You sleep in the bedroom and I'll sleep out here."

She nodded but continued to stall, a look of

uncertainty on her face. He turned her in the right direction, put a hand to the small of her back, and led the way. At the door, he flipped the light switch, brightening the room.

Steps muffled by the thick rug covering the wooden floor, he left her at the edge of the bed centered in the room. Turning for the dresser shoved against the opposite wall, he pulled out the sleepshirt she'd bought.

His first intention was to help. He stepped back to the bed, the shirt dangling from his finger. As he offered it to her, he realized the mistake he was making.

Seeing her naked would do no good. It was hard enough keeping his hands off her when she was fully dressed. The temptation would be too great if given the opportunity to see her without her clothes.

She grabbed the shirt and hugged it tightly to her middle. Uncertainty flashed in her eyes.

He fought back the need to reach for her. "If you need me, I'll be in the other room."

She nodded, still clutching her shirt.

He knew it was time to go. Leaning down, he pressed a feather light kiss to her lips. "Sweet dreams, princess."

Chapter Ten

From the front porch, Hunter watched the sun peek over the horizon. He cradled a cup of coffee in his hands, while savoring the brilliant streaks of crimson and ruby stretching across the sky.

When was the last time he'd enjoyed a sunrise? Since joining the Bureau, he hadn't spent much time on the simple pleasures in life. His theory had always been, work as hard and long as possible. It kept him busy and kept his mind off things better left forgotten.

When he'd left Denver, he placed his energy and determination into reaching his career goals. He'd been young, enthusiastic, exactly what the Bureau was looking for. They'd seen in him a man willing to put his life into his job. A man who held no other importance other than his position as an agent.

It was the life he'd chosen. The life he'd return to as soon as this thing with Paxton was over.

Paxton. Her name was enough to bring his senses alert. He had believed he'd get a better sleep than the night before since they were no longer sharing a bed.

He'd been wrong.

Even with the walls separating them, he was aware of her. He pictured her cuddled up in bed, honey-blond hair fanning out behind her while her firm, rounded breasts rose and fell with each breath. She looked like an angel when she slept, he knew that. It took everything he had not to sneak in and join her.

Last night, he'd slipped again, letting old feelings get the best of him. He'd gotten too close, wanting to comfort her fears, ease the tension from her body.

But, this morning, with the bright light of day dawning, he knew better. Letting her back into his heart, his soul, would be the worst thing he could do. There was no hope for them. There never had been.

Even if he could forget the pain of the past it wouldn't change the fact they came from two completely different worlds. Their backgrounds blended about as well as oil and water. She knew nothing of the way he lived. He knew nothing of her ways.

Had he not been a young man foolishly in love the last time, he'd have known better than to get involved with her. He was older now, wiser. He knew he and Paxton together was an impossible dream. There was nothing between them. Nothing strong enough to bind them together, regardless of their differences.

They didn't have it in the past, and they didn't have it now.

His emotional wall firmly in place, he enjoyed the remainder of the sunrise. When the door creaked open, he paid it no attention. The smarter, more reserved Hunter was back. The sooner Paxton realized that, the better.

****

She hadn't bothered changing out of her nightshirt before looking for Hunter. Joining him on the front porch, the cold morning air sent a wave of goose bumps over bared limbs.

The weather, though, was nothing compared to the

chill she felt when he looked her way.

Gone was the tender, gentle man who'd helped calm her worries and left her with a soft goodnight kiss, carrying her into dreams. There was nothing soft or gentle in the hardened look he shot her way or the grim set of his lips.

"When I couldn't find you inside, I got a little worried." Paxton folded her arms over her chest to fight off the chill of both the weather and the man at her side.

"There's nothing to be worried about." His voice was matter-of-fact. "We're safe here. At least for the time being."

Safe was a term easily argued as far as she was concerned. They may be safe from Grant, but she wasn't safe from Hunter or the effect he had on her.

Her dreams had overflowed with his image. She'd fallen into sleep with the feel of his lips on hers and craving the comfort of his arms.

Her resolve was slipping and she was helpless to fight it. Her heart was beginning to ache again for what she couldn't have.

Sometime during the dark hours of the night, she'd come to realize it was time she told him the truth about their final day together. She owed him that much after all he was doing, risking, to keep her safe.

The truth wouldn't change things, she was smart enough to realize that. But she hoped it would help heal her buried wounds as well as his own. If they could make it over this final step between them, maybe she'd have a better chance at surviving the second round of good-byes she knew would be coming.

"We should get into town relatively early." His deep voice startled her. He turned for the door, resting his hand on the knob. "It would be best to get there before the tourists start coming around."

"Are you still worried somebody might actually recognize me?"

Her question stopped him before he had a chance to disappear inside. He turned back, dark eyes cold and harsh. "In my line of work, we don't take any risks, no matter how slim they might be. It might be a long shot somebody recognizes you, but there is no way we can be certain they won't."

He was right. No matter how outrageous it seemed that somebody this far out of her social circle would recognize her. Just a couple days ago, she'd believed it outrageous her fiancé could be wanted by the FBI. That he was a killer who was out to hurt her.

Following him inside, she went after the scent of fresh coffee from the kitchen. Pouring a cup, she calculated how long it had been since Hunter had taken her from her wedding.

Though it felt like a lifetime ago, it had actually been less than a week since the chaos began. She thought of her father. The worry he must have. If only there was a way to ease his mind and let him know she was okay.

She thought of asking Hunter to let her use his phone, but knew what his answer would be. He'd just finished telling her he didn't take unnecessary risks. She was sure he'd consider contacting her father a risk.

There might be another way. Sipping on her coffee, watching Hunter refill his own, an idea took root inside her head. They were going into town. There had to be telephones there. If she could slip away for just a minute, then maybe—

She tucked the idea down when he stepped in front of her with a curious look. "You okay?" His hand drifted from his side before dropping back to place. "You looked lost there for a minute."

"I'm fine," she nodded. "I was just thinking of some things that might be good to pick up for dinner while we're in town."

"I think we're safest sticking to canned and frozen foods. Neither of us are much for cooking."

She planted her hands firmly on her sides. "I'll have you know, I've been cooking for myself for some time."

"What happened to Macy?" He recalled the woman who'd worked for the Walsh family since the day Paxton was born.

"She's still around, but what good does it do me. I don't live with my father anymore. I haven't for eight years."

"You moved out from under Daddy's wing?" He shook his head in disbelief.

He still saw her as the spoiled little rich girl she'd once been. She bristled at the thought. He'd grown, matured, over the years. Didn't it make sense she would do the same?

"I have my own place. My own job."

"You work?" The shock in his voice matched his wide-eyed stare.

"Volunteer work. But it still demands a good fifty hours a week."

His expression was a mixture of disbelief and awe. Somewhere in there, she thought she saw the tiniest bit of admiration as well.

Why should she care what he thought of her? It

shouldn't bother her that he didn't expect to hear she'd made a life of her own. A life away from her father's protective hold.

But it did. It was hard to accept the truth. He still saw her as the eighteen-year-old girl she'd been, spoiled and naive. He hadn't thought her capable of growth, maturity, and was obviously surprised she'd accomplished both.

He swept up next to her and rinsed his cup in the sink. His nearness sent heat racing through her limbs.

"So what is it that you do?" He leaned back against the counter, folding his long arms over his chest. Standing in front of the only window in the kitchen, the morning sun highlighted the short ends of his black hair and softened his rough appearance.

Fighting to hold on to control and not lose herself in the sight of him, she turned and rinsed her own cup. "I work at a place called Grayson House. It's a club designed to keep teenagers off the streets. I plan their activities, counsel them, and challenge them to be their best."

"You volunteer your days to work with a bunch of troubled teenagers?" He shook his head. "That's not what I would have pictured."

She could tell him the truth. Tell him he was the reason she dedicated so much of her life to making sure the kids she worked with had a chance in life.

She could tell him, but knew she wouldn't.

"Sounds to me like many of your assumptions about me are wrong." She stepped away from the sink. "I guess you figured you were the only one allowed to grow and move on with your life."

He stopped her with a firm hand on her arm,

turning her around to face him. "With your last goodbye, you didn't give me any reason to think differently."

"I was eighteen. A kid. In those months we were together, did you really believe I was shallow enough to stay that way for the rest of my life?"

He crowded closer, his warm breath fanning over her face. "It doesn't matter now, does it, princess. Whatever was between us is long gone. Our past has nothing to do with what we have become."

Oh, but it did. It had everything to do with who they were. She knew that as surely as she knew her own name. The precious time they'd spent together, the bitter ending between them, chiseled a path for them to follow for the rest of their lives.

She was a different person because of Hunter. She knew he was different because of her as well. They might not be good changes, but they were there, shaping them in many ways.

Abruptly, he stepped back, stuffing his hands into the front pockets of his jeans. "We're wasting our time. Go get ready. We'll leave in thirty minutes."

She didn't want to leave him just yet. They'd touched on their past, and she wanted to dig further. It was there on the tip of her tongue to tell him the truth about what happened. But one look at his stony expression changed her mind.

Now was not the time. As much as she wanted it to be, she knew he'd stop her cold if she tried to say anything.

"Thirty minutes," she repeated with a stern nod of her head. "I'll be ready."

****

The ride into town was silent. It seemed the more Paxton became aware of Hunter the more he closed himself away. He'd shoved a wedge between them since she found him on the porch that morning, and he clearly didn't intend to remove it.

Dressed in blue denim jeans and a dark-red collared shirt, he was hard to ignore, especially in the close confines of the Cherokee. Every time he moved, she caught a flash of red in the corner of her eye. Each breath he took filtered in her direction, making her aware of him so close at her side.

Well...she wasn't about to spend the day acting like some lovesick teenager. She'd already played that role once. Squaring her shoulders, she decided it was time to copy his coldness. If he wanted to keep things distant between them, she would gladly comply.

"Almost there," he announced as they topped the incline in the road. Below sat a scattering of dark wood and redbrick buildings. Most looked like they dated back to the turn of the century.

The closer they came, the more she noticed the old west appeal. Stores and businesses along the main street were constructed from long slats of aged pine and oak. Wooden signs hung from hooks. Old, battered shingles covered slanted roofs. Barrels lined the dusty sidewalk. Some of them were empty while others overflowed with bright, colorful flowers.

Hunter pulled to a stop in front of a small store crammed in the middle of the street. The wooden sign displayed the words, *Keller's Market*, in white, bold letters. Two older men, both with pipes poking from their mouths, occupied a small bench in front of the store. They nodded as she and Hunter passed through the front door.

The silver bell above the door jingled with their arrival. From behind the counter, a gray-haired man glanced up from the newspaper spread in front of him, offering a quick wave before returning to his reading.

"I don't think you had to worry about me being recognized in a place like this." She tapped the baseball cap he insisted she wear again. Pinching the bridge of her sunglasses between her forefinger and thumb, she eased them off her face.

"The town isn't awake yet. It might not look like much on the outside but this is a tourist hot spot for those on their way to or leaving Yellowstone. The old west charm brings them here in droves."

"Sounds like you've been here often." She tried ignoring the sharp pain that came with knowing, in so many ways, he was a stranger to her. She had no idea where the last ten years had taken him or the life he'd led.

He shrugged, leading them down a small aisle filled with canned goods. "As I said, a friend of mine owns the cabin. On occasion, when I need to get away, I come here for some rest."

Without warning, images formed of another woman sharing the same cabin with him. There was no reason to believe she was the only female he'd taken there. It was a romantic little place, private, and remote. What better surroundings could a man ask for when trying to sweep a woman off her feet?

She hadn't thought of it. Hadn't allowed herself to think of Hunter with someone else. She wasn't dumb. She knew he hadn't spent the last ten years pining away for her. He didn't wear a ring, so she assumed he wasn't married. But she hadn't asked about girlfriends who might be back home waiting for him.

She turned away, not wanting him to see her stumble over the ache in her heart. She couldn't believe how deep the hurt was when she thought of him with someone else.

It wasn't like she had a claim over him. She, herself, was supposed to be married to another man by now. Any, and all, attachments to Hunter had been severed long ago.

But, damn, it hurt to think about. Her heart ached as she pictured him wrapped tenderly around another woman as he whispered the same loving words he'd once given her.

"The cabin must be a romantic getaway," she forced out through the lump in her throat. With shaking hands, she reached for a can of vegetable soup, afraid to look at him.

"I wouldn't know," his voice came from over her shoulder. "This is the first time I haven't been alone up here."

He reached past her, grabbed a couple cans of chili, dumping them into the basket before moving on. Deep breaths helped chase away her emotions. She had no right to the questions running through her head. His life was his own.

Staring at the hard muscles of his back, she forced her thoughts to more pressing issues. This, more than likely, would be her only chance at finding a telephone. She only hoped somewhere inside the tiny store there was one to be found.

Together, they worked their way through the store, each tossing their own selections into the cart as they scanned the aisles. A calm easiness surrounded them, as if they had done this sort of thing together for years. To unknowing eyes, they looked like nothing more than a couple out grocery shopping together.

Was this how they would have been had they not parted? So many times in her dreams, she'd seen her and Hunter married with a family. So many times, she'd imagined what it would have been like to be his wife. What life would have held in store if she hadn't told him goodbye on that fateful day.

"I think we've got all that we're going to need." His deep voice floated over her. Turning, he led them back to the front counter. The clerk set down his paper to ring up their purchases.

"Excuse me." She leaned over the counter. His attention strayed away from the cash register, settling on her.

"May I help you?"

"I was wondering where your restroom was." She carefully kept her gaze away from Hunter's, afraid with a look he'd know what she had planned.

An old gnarled finger stuck out toward the back of the store. "Back that way. Can't miss the big sign leading the way."

"Thank you." She turned.

"Maybe I should go along with you." Hunter stopped her before she took a step.

Inhaling a deep breath before facing him, she hoped her expression didn't show her nervousness. "I'll be fine. I don't think there's any threat to worry about here."

He didn't agree right away, and she held her breath, waiting.

His eyes darted around the store, from the front door to the back wall where the restrooms were located. "I suppose you'll be all right. Just be sure you make it quick."

She nodded, waiting until she was out of sight before exhaling a relieved sigh. Time was of the essence now. It wouldn't take long for him to come looking for her. She was sure, even now, he'd glanced at his watch, timing her. Hopefully, if luck was with her, she'd be back before he grew suspicious.

As the clerk promised, a large bathroom sign pointed down a small, dim hallway. She crossed her fingers, turning into the hallway, and almost shouted with joy when she came upon the old pay telephone hanging on the wall. Her guess had paid off.

With her heart beating a frantic pace against her ribs, she cradled the receiver between her ear and shoulder. Seconds later, she had a call sent through to her father's house. While she waited for him to pick up, she angled her hip against the hard wall. From there she had a good view of the store. There was no way Hunter could come up on her without her knowing it.

"Walsh residence," her father's voice filled the line. Hearing the familiar sound was enough to threaten an onslaught of tears. She held them back, not wanting to worry him.

"Dad," she spoke quietly though she knew Hunter couldn't hear her from the front of the store.

"Paxton." Her name escaped on a note of worry and fear. "Are you all right?"

"I'm fine."

"Where are you? What happened?" His questions came in a rush. With a deep breath, she stole a glance at the store then turned her concentration to the call.

"I can't explain right now." She knew her time was limited. "When I get home, I'll tell you everything."

"What do you mean you can't explain," her father demanded. "Grant and I have been worried sick. I hate thinking of you out there alone. Imagining what could happen to you without anyone looking after you."

She tried not to bristle at her father's overprotective ramblings. It was something she was used to.

He was convinced she needed to be constantly taken care of. That she was nothing without a man looking out for her. In his eyes, she was a small, lost child, needing to be led around by the hand.

"I'm not alone. I have somebody with me."

"Who?" The single word burst through the line. She felt like a teenager again, facing her father's demands.

"Somebody I can trust. That's all that matters."

"Enough of this foolishness." The worry in his voice quickly changed to anger. "Tell me where you are. Whom you're with. I won't be left in the dark."

She knew the seconds ticked away. Much longer and Hunter would come looking for her. Any minute now, she expected him to step into the hallway. She couldn't let that happen.

"Paxton, talk to me," her father demanded.

"I'm with Hunter." She braced herself for what she knew was coming.

"You're with who?" Her father's roar blasted over the line. "You're with that Hunter Reese fellow? I thought he was long gone."

"It's a long story that I don't have time to explain

right now."

"Where are you? Why are you with him? He already tried ruining your life once. I didn't think you were foolish enough to make the same mistake twice."

She wasn't going to get in this argument with him. "Look, Dad, I really need to go. I just wanted to call and let you know I was all right."

"Don't you hang up until you tell me where you are."

"I'm in a little town outside of Yellowstone. I'm staying at a cabin that belongs to a friend of Hunter's."

There was a rustling at the other end. "Give me directions. I'll send Grant after you."

"No." The single word came out in a stubborn tone. "I don't want him knowing where I am. I don't even want him to know I called."

"What nonsense is this? He needs to know you called and that you're all right. He's been worried sick. He calls at least three times a day, wondering if I've heard from you."

Frustration setting in, she pinched the bridge of her nose, fighting the headache threatening to explode. Maybe this wasn't such a good idea after all.

"As your daughter, I'm asking you not to tell him a thing. I need you to understand, he can't know anything about me. Please, Dad. Do this one thing for me."

"Paxton, wait—"

"I can't. I have to go. I'm counting on you to do as I asked. I promise I'll explain everything as soon as I get back."

Her father's demands echoed on the other end as she replaced the receiver. Her hands trembled and she clasped them tightly in front of her.

She hoped her father would do as she asked. At times, he was hard to get through to, but she prayed his daughter's plea would win out against any tactics Grant might use. Hopefully, he heard the desperation in her voice.

There was still no movement outside the tiny hallway. She thanked her lucky stars she hadn't been found out. Hunter wouldn't like it in the least bit if he learned he'd been lied to. The thought of his dark, angry face was enough to send a shiver up her spine.

Dragging in a long breath of air, she struggled to get herself back in order. The littlest mistake would give him reason to doubt her. She didn't need to spend the rest of the day trying to explain her reasons for contacting her father. Especially now, when she worried if she'd done more harm than good.

Chapter Eleven

Hunter's gaze remained glued on the back of the store where Paxton disappeared.

Where was she?

"Sir, your change." The man behind the counter waved a hand of bills to grab his attention. With a forced smile, he turned back, accepted the money, and stuffed it into his wallet.

"Can I keep these here for a minute?" He rested a palm on top of the white, plastic bags holding their food.

"Fine with me." The clerk buried his nose in the thick newspaper as Hunter turned away from the counter.

His steps were quick as he started for the back of the store. A nagging worry tickled at the back of his mind. He was sure they were safe, sure there was no way Grant could find them. Yet, Paxton's absence had him on edge, second-guessing his decision to let her go alone.

He was almost at a run when she stepped out of a small hallway to his right. With one quick look, he knew his worry had been for nothing. She was fine.

"Sorry it took so long." Her eyes never met his face. Long lashes cast shadows against her cheek, hiding away whatever secrets she held. Twisting her hands awkwardly, she moved ahead of him.

Suspicion spiked. He'd handled too many nervous criminals not to know she was hiding something. But what could she hide with a trip to the bathroom? There wasn't much chance to get into trouble.

Still, something caused her hands to tremble and her expression to close up. Something had happened she didn't want him to know about, and his gut instinct told him to find out what it was. He didn't like secrets or having things hidden from him.

Hanging back as she hurried forward, he took a step back, getting a better look down the hallway, searching for an answer to what she might have been doing. He saw nothing that spiked his interest and, with a low, muttered curse, followed after her.

"What took so long?" He caught up with her at the front of the store, stopping long enough to gather their bags before breaking out into the bright, morning sun.

From the corner of his eye, he watched as she nibbled on her bottom lip. "I got distracted."

"Uh, huh." He tossed their bags into the back of the Cherokee before joining her in the front seat. He waited until they were on their way out of town before saying another word.

"I can't help but wonder what there is to distract someone inside a bathroom. Seems to me it's all pretty much the basic stuff inside there."

"I…uh…"

"You what?"

"I just got lost in my thoughts." Her voice took on a sharp edge. "I can't help it if this mess has me running in circles. I was trying to get myself back together before I came out, that's all."

That's all. He shook his head. He didn't believe her

for a minute, but Paxton stiffened as if ready for a fight, and he had no urge to go down that path again.

He'd find out what she was hiding in that pretty little head of hers. He had no doubt about that. Maybe she thought she had him where she wanted him. He'd show her there was no hiding things from him. It rubbed against him wrong when people didn't open up and tell the truth.

He asked nothing else and let silence fill the Cherokee. Sensing her relief, he wondered even more what she was hiding.

At the cabin, they unloaded the groceries, working around one another in the tiny confines of the kitchen. Her scent drifted around him, reminding him of things better left forgotten. He tightened when her thigh brushed against him as she reached over his head to stack the canned goods.

His earlier resolve was quickly shattered. Every time he convinced himself he could hold his own around her, she crumbled whatever control he had.

"I guess I can get rid of this." She grabbed the rim of her cap, tossing it carelessly across the table. Tumbles of honey-blond hair fell over her shoulders. Reaching up, she tucked an errant strand behind her ear.

He took a step forward. That undeniable bond that had existed between them wasn't as far gone as he believed. With her every move, he made one of his own in her direction, drawn to her in a way he was powerless to fight.

She clasped her hands above her head, lengthening her arms in a full body stretch that he was sure was going to be the death of him. Her breasts pushed out in invitation. A small sliver of ivory skin peeked from the edge of her shorts.

He stepped closer. The delicate aroma of honeysuckle blanketed the air, drawing him to the beauty standing before him. He knew each step he took was dangerous. Dangerous to himself as well as to his promise to keep a distance from the woman who'd broken his heart so long ago.

Her arms dropped back to her sides, eyes widening in surprise when she realized how close he stood. Hovering over her, he said nothing, his expression dark, clouded. He didn't move, could hardly breath, as he struggled to break free.

He wanted to kiss her. He wanted to wrap her in his arms and never let go. There were memories he'd never forgotten from the time they'd spent together. Memories of passions that had never died. His body called out for those memories, begging for release in the sweeping heat of desire they once shared.

He was there. So close. All he had to do was reach out, take her, and claim her as his own. His hands lifted, reached for her.

The sharp cry of an animal outside broke through the silence, shattering the spell. It was enough distraction to pull him back. His hands fell to his sides without ever touching her. The scent of honeysuckle lingered, but he found the strength to back away and put much needed distance between them.

For a second, he held her with his eyes then turned on his heels, storming out of the kitchen without a word.

****

Curling into the corner of the couch, Paxton grabbed the mystery novel she'd found earlier that day.

She was already halfway through. With another day like today she'd be done.

After the strange episode with Hunter in the kitchen, he'd disappeared. They hadn't shared a room since, and she found herself with a lot of time on her hands so she'd decided to explore the cabin. It was small, but she'd made the best of it until she'd found the novel, tucked away in a closet, and figured it was a great way to pass the time.

Only once was she pulled away from the unfolding story. A rumble of hunger in her stomach forced her to stir up dinner, which Hunter ate in the front room while she remained in the kitchen. With clean up done, she was ready to waste the remaining hours until bed hidden inside her book.

She barely made it through a page when the opposite end of the couch sagged. Glancing over the top of the book, she watched Hunter push as far into the other corner as he could.

He didn't look her way or acknowledge she was there. He kept his focus on the fire he'd stoked to life, lost in the flames. She felt his tension from where she sat, saw it in the tight muscles of his arms, and the hard set of his cold expression.

He was proving to be more of a mystery than the novel she was reading. His behavior since they'd returned from town was strange. There was a point when she'd been sure he was about to kiss her. But before she'd been able to prepare herself he'd turned and walked away.

After that, he avoided her, saying not a single word in the hours that passed. So why was he here now? Why join her on the couch? Unable to read his thoughts left her full of questions.

He shifted in place but still didn't turn to look at her. Watching, waiting for him to do or say something was driving her crazy. Fighting back the urge to force him to talk, she turned back to her book.

The words swirled before her eyes, making no sense inside her jumbled brain. She made it through an entire page then realized she had no idea what she'd read.

She was unable to focus on the story, yet she was more than capable of noticing every little movement Hunter made. When he lifted his hand to run his fingers through his ebony hair, she watched through the corner of her eye, noticing each rise and fall of his chest as he sucked in even breaths.

Pulling her attention back to the book, she read over the page she'd finished, forcing away thoughts of the dark, brooding man at her side. Picking out each word, she read with great care, stubbornly keeping herself from straying again.

Wood crackling in the fire was the only sound in the room. When the deep baritone of Hunter's voice broke through the silence, she jumped in surprise, the book slipping from her fingers, and falling to the floor.

"Did you love him?" He didn't turn away from the fire. He simply sat, waiting for an answer.

"Did I love Grant?"

He nodded, his gray eyes meeting hers as he turned away from the fire. There was an intensity in his expression she hadn't expected. She wondered how much her answer meant to him.

"I agreed to marry him, didn't I?"

He shook his head. "That doesn't answer my

question. Loving him and marrying him are two different things."

"Funny," she shrugged. "I always thought they went together."

He moved away from his side of the couch, coming to rest in the center cushion between them. His thigh brushed hers. His spicy masculine scent washed over her. He was close. Too close. She curled further into her corner of the couch.

"Tell me." A dark shadow slid over his face. "Tell me you loved him. That he was everything to you. That he made your heart beat and your body tingle."

It was almost frightening, the way he loomed over her, demanding answers he had no right to. For a moment, she couldn't speak, couldn't move out of the trance he held her under. Gathering her senses, she opened her mouth to answer then snapped it shut before saying a word.

She was going to lie and tell him that she'd loved Grant. Something inside wouldn't let her. Instead, she shook her head. "No. I never loved him." She stared at the floor rather than meeting his eyes.

Hunter's finger hooked underneath her chin, pulling her gaze to his. "Then why?" His voice lost the edge from before. "Why did you agree to marry him if you didn't love him?"

How could she make him understand? How could she explain that even as a grown woman, she still did her best to abide by her father's wishes? Grant was perfect husband material in her father's eyes. He was everything Theodore Walsh had ever wanted for his daughter.

After ten long years of never feeling the way she

had when she was with Hunter, Paxton gave up on childish dreams of happily ever after. She had no illusions when she'd agreed to marry Grant. She had grown, matured. She knew she was agreeing to spend the rest of her life being comfortable in her relationship.

She couldn't admit that to Hunter though. "Marriage is more than love."

"Since when?"

"You can't be that dense." She shook her head, sending honey-blond hair tumbling over her shoulders. "People are always marrying for reasons other than love. There's companionship, reliability, comfort. There are many reasons why people get married. They don't always include love."

"I'm not talking about other people." He leaned forward, bringing his face within an inch of hers. "I'm talking about you. The Paxton I knew would have never agreed to spend the rest of her life with a man she didn't love."

Her heart pounded against her ribs, the beat so loud she was sure he heard it. He was too close. Too threatening. She wanted nothing more than to shrink away and run from the fire he ignited inside each time he was near.

"The Paxton you knew went away a long time ago."

He shook his head, dark eyes piercing through her soul as if he could read the secrets hidden away inside. "I don't believe you. I don't believe you changed enough to want to spend the rest of your life with a man you didn't love."

Why was he pushing? Why did he care why she agreed to marry Grant? It wasn't his concern.

He leaned closer, his breath a warm feather against her cheek. "Tell me the truth. Tell me why you were planning to say, I do, to a man you didn't love."

"Because—" she started then stalled. She couldn't tell him. Didn't want to tell him.

Eyes, as stormy as a cloudy sky, probed through her resistance. Reaching up, he cupped her cheek in his palm. "Tell me."

"Because I knew I'd never be able to love another man." The words escaped with a painful stab. "Because, after you, my heart wasn't open to another. I knew I'd never find love again so I settled for something less."

Tears choked the back of her throat. She wasn't going to cry. She hadn't cried for what she'd lost in many years. The pain had been tucked away deep inside where she didn't have to face it day after day.

Holding her with his stormy gaze, time seemed to stop. She heard nothing of the wind pushing against the windows or the fire crackling in the hearth a few feet away. Her senses were aware only of Hunter's heavy breathing and the painful beat of her heart.

His hands cupped her face in a hold meant to keep her still so she was a captive to his stare. "I would have given you the world and more." His mouth brushed against hers. "I would have given you my very life if you asked for it."

Pain, unlike any she'd ever seen from him, sliced through his expression, stabbing into her soul. He might have tried to hide it, but he was still hurting. She'd hurt him worse than she ever thought possible.

A tear escaped to slide down her cheek. His angry glare focused on that single tear and her breath caught as he used the pad of his thumb to wipe it away. "Don't. I don't want your tears."

Her sapphire eyes, misty with unshed tears, met his. She felt his anger. The heat rolling off him. She wasn't sure what she should say—what she should do. They traveled down a road they'd left unpaved years ago, and she wasn't sure she liked the route they were taking.

The minutes felt like hours as anger and betrayal simmered between them. She sat motionless, unsure of what was to come. With each heated second he stared at her, his expression grew darker, stormier.

"Damn you." His harsh voice broke through the eerie silence. "Damn you for making me still want you after you stole away everything there was between us."

His lips closed over hers, punishing her for what she had done. His hands fisted in her hair, holding her almost painfully to his kiss. He was trying to hurt her just as she had hurt him. His kiss, his hold, was not of tenderness and love. It sparked with anger and frustration.

Bruising her soft lips, he forced her mouth to open. She knew she should break away, but she couldn't do it. Instead, she met his kiss with the same fierce response as desperation and need swelled around her.

He groaned low and hard, his hands releasing their hold on her hair, skimming down her body. They circled around her slender waist. Pulling her flush against him, he rubbed her against the bulge threatening to break through his jeans. His fingers pushed into her skin, holding her where he wanted her.

It was getting out of control. She knew it, but her body called out over reason, begging to be satisfied.

She clasped his broad shoulders, holding on for dear life. She pressed against the firm lines of his chest, her breasts rubbing against him, thighs stroking his. Awareness sparked between her legs where he continued to rub fiercely against her.

His mouth left hers, nipping her bottom lip before searing a trail down the curve of her neck. Through the thin material of her shirt, he found a pointed nipple, sucking it between his teeth until she gasped in a mixture of pain and desire. One hand trailed from her waist, cupping where he had been rubbing only seconds before.

"Tell me you've missed this," he demanded. "Tell me no other man can take you the way I can."

She squirmed against him, desperate to release the passion swirling through. She ached for release. Pleaded for it with her body smashed against his.

"Tell me." His teeth sank into her neck, demanding an answer.

"Only you." Her nails dug into his back. "Only you can make me feel this way."

His long arms came around her in a desperate hold. He captured her mouth with a low, satisfied grumble. Beneath her, he shifted his hips to ride against her, the denim between them doing little to quench the fire burning there.

She wanted him. Wanted this. It felt so right. This was where she belonged—had always belonged. Her body was starving for the passion he offered.

She clung desperately to his hard muscles while his mouth assaulted her with a raging kiss. She didn't ever want to let go. Didn't ever want this moment to end.

"Hunter," his name escaped on a frantic gasp of air

as his hand squeezed between them. His fingers caressed her through her shorts, pushing her higher until she was sure she'd explode.

Passion spiraled, coiling through her limbs. She was ready to give him all of her. Ready to find the special spark that existed only between the two of them.

With a curse, he tore his mouth away, and left her struggling to catch a breath. For a second, he held her gaze then lifted her up and off of him. The sudden separation sent a shiver up her spine. Wrapping her arms across her front, she fought off the chill.

Before her eyes, he closed himself off as his expression grew as cold as stone. "Go to bed," he ordered without meeting her eyes, diverting his attention to the fire. "Before we do something we'll both regret."

She was helpless to protest. On wobbly legs, she pushed from the couch, looking down on him, a million questions running through her mind.

He didn't acknowledge her, though he was aware of her eyes on him. Before she made a fool of herself and begged for his attention, she turned toward the bedroom. Closing the door tightly behind her, she fell onto the bed and pulled the pillow over her head, hiding away from the harsh realities of the world around her.

Chapter Twelve

What in the world was he thinking?

The question waged a vicious war inside Hunter's head through the night and was back with just as much force with the dawning of the new day. He could count maybe two hours of real sleep. The rest of the night, he tossed and turned on the uncomfortable couch, desperately trying to clear the image of Paxton from his mind.

What in the world was I thinking?

Pushing from the couch with a violent shove, he stormed to the coffeepot, bringing the aroma of fresh brewed coffee into the tiny cabin within minutes. He'd called himself a fool many times throughout the night and was on the same track this morning as he stood at the small kitchen window, staring outside.

Hands clenched behind his back, his shoulders tight, he fought the anger and frustration, two emotions he was used to experiencing since Paxton was back in his life. He let things get out of hand the night before, almost losing control when he knew better.

His body ached, desperate for release since Paxton's tender body had been captured underneath his. His need for her was so extreme it was painful. Denying that need had almost killed him.

"Morning." The soft whisper of her voice drew him away from the window. Reluctant, he turned, coming face to face with a sleep-tousled angel.

She stood at the edge of the kitchen, hair ruffled in untamed curls, cheeks stained red from sleep. Her oversized sleepshirt clung to her curves. One side slipped off her shoulder, exposing the creamy white skin beneath.

His strangled emotions swelled with renewed force. How was he supposed to resist such temptation? Where in the world was he going to find the strength to keep away from the beauty who'd haunted his dreams for ten years?

"Coffee's made." He jerked his head toward the coffeepot. Without offering to pour her a cup, he filled his own and moved to the other side of the kitchen.

He was going to go crazy if he stayed inside the cabin with her all day, but there was no other option. They couldn't risk going back into town, and the dark clouds hovering outside hinted at a summer storm creeping in. He had no choice but to stay inside where her sweet scent would tease him all day long.

"Hunter." Her voice broke through his thoughts. She stood, hip resting softly against the counter, and hands cradling her coffee cup. "About last night—"

His hand shot up before she could finish. "Last night was a mistake I don't intend to repeat. What happened was a slip of better judgment. I can assure you it won't happen again.

Over the rim of her cup, her sapphire eyes shifted with hurt. He felt a stab of guilt for being the one to cause it, but it had to be done. He had to make it clear such mistakes wouldn't be repeated.

He knew better than to get involved all over again. Nothing good would come out of it. They were still two different people from two different backgrounds. Their lives didn't belong together. Becoming involved would only open him back up to the same heartache he'd experienced before when he'd believed their differences didn't matter.

"Look." He set his cup on the counter and ran an aggravated hand through his dark hair. "Let's just keep our distance as best as we can. It won't do us any good to be together after what happened last night."

He scooted past, disappearing from the kitchen. Gathering a change of clothes into his arms, he locked himself away in the bathroom. A long, hot shower, he hoped, would clear away the tension, the pain, lingering long after his time with Paxton.

****

Like she could avoid him in a place this small.

Through the morning and afternoon, Paxton found it impossible to keep her distance. His presence loomed around every corner. The heat of his body filled every room. He was crazy if he thought they could carry on like this forever.

He was even crazier if he truly believed they could forget what happened between them. The memory of what they came so close to sharing lingered in the air. The mere sight of the couch sent her blood to boiling.

Outside, the rain that had fallen in a soft pattern throughout the day, picked up intensity, pounding a stucco beat against the windows. Wind pushed against the log walls, whistling through the cracks.

It was dreary outside, and inside—the atmosphere felt no different. She couldn't control the storm Mother Nature raged, but she could do something about the dark cloud hovering within the cabin. If Hunter wanted to walk around in doom and gloom that was up to him. As for her, she'd had enough. It was time to bring some light into the day, or at least what was left of it.

Rummaging inside the refrigerator, she piled her arms with the fixings for cold-cut sandwiches. Grabbing a bag of bagels off the counter, she set to work on her famous bagel sandwiches. A meal she'd perfected her first year living on her own.

After the sandwiches were prepared and arranged on a platter she'd found in the cupboard, she turned her concentration to cutting up fresh fruit, layering it in a deep dish. Some bagged chips, a pitcher of iced tea, and her meal was complete.

Remembering the blankets she'd spotted in the back closet, she dragged out a patterned flannel throw and smoothed it out in front of the fire. She tossed two large pillows from the couch on top of the blanket, scooting them to opposite corners with the tips of her toes.

Scurrying back into the kitchen, she collected the sandwiches and fruit, and placed them in the center of the blanket. Straightening, she turned back to retrieve the chips and iced tea, but Hunter's looming form blocked her path.

"What are you doing?" With one shoulder leaning against the wall, he folded his arms over his chest, and eyed the layout in front of the fire.

"Dinner." She brushed past, gathered the remaining food. When she returned, he still stared at the arrangement on the floor, his eyes showing anything but pleasure at what she planned.

Making a great show of pouring the iced tea into two glasses, tearing open the bag of chips, she made herself comfortable on one of the cushions. "I thought an indoor picnic would be a nice contrast to the weather." She reached over and grabbed a bagel sandwich from the platter. "It's a simple dinner, but it's good."

He was reluctant to join her, his gaze sweeping from the blanket, to the food, to her. "Why can't we just eat at the table like normal people?"

She took a bite from her sandwich, refusing to wait on him before feeding her hungry stomach. "If that's what you would rather do, go ahead. I'm not going to force you to sit down with me."

He looked from the kitchen, to her, then back to the kitchen. Without letting on that she was tensely waiting for his decision, she took another bite, washing it down with a slow drink from her glass.

Seconds later, he joined her on the blanket, mumbling something under his breath that she figured was best she didn't hear. The light of the fire silhouetted him from behind, casting a shadow over his disturbing presence.

Maybe this hadn't been such a good idea after all. Instead of easing the mood between them as she'd hoped, her little setup on the floor seemed to strengthen the tension. It was too intimate. A little too romantic. Visions of another picnic—one they had shared beside a gently rolling stream—filled her head.

It had been a soft, summer day with birds chirping in the trees and a gentle breeze carrying the scent of wildflowers through the air. They ate side by side, unable to keep their hands off one another. Afterwards, a dip in the warm water of the stream left them clinging to one another, hands roaming over slick skin, and mouths tasting the water drops that beaded against their skin.

She remembered falling to the ground, stretching out on the grassy knoll, and burying themselves in the blue flowers brushing against their ankles only seconds before. With the roar of the stream at their side and the bright blue of the sky above, they'd surrendered to their passion, taking pleasure from one another repeatedly.

With a silent groan, she pushed the images out of her mind. Concentrating on the orange slice she gathered in her hand, she waited until she was sure all signs of her memories were gone before daring a glance in Hunter's direction.

He had one of the bagel sandwiches grasped in his strong hands, a large bite already taken out of the side. It didn't appear old memories had come back to haunt him. He seemed more relaxed in front of the fire than he had all day. Reaching out, he shoved his hand into the open bag of chips.

At least one of them was enjoying themselves. This little picnic had been her idea, but it looked like Hunter was getting the most pleasure out of it while she fought away thoughts from the past.

He stretched his long legs out, toes only inches away from her crossed legs. Settling his hands over his full stomach, his attention strayed to the dancing flames at his side.

In the time it had taken her to finish a sandwich, a couple slices of oranges, he'd made his way through two sandwiches, a handful of chips and half the fruit inside the large bowl. For someone who was reluctant to join her, he sure took none of that reluctance out on his food. A satisfied smile graced his lips while a long, hearty sigh escaped.

Pushing up from her pillow, she began gathering the dishes.

"Leave them." He tugged on her hand, pulling her back down to the blanket. Gone was the man who'd set her straight about the two of them that morning in the kitchen. The food seemed to have gentled his harsh declarations about the mandatory distance between them.

Tucking her knees underneath her chin and wrapping her arms around her shins, she stared at the brilliant reds and oranges spiraling through the fire.

"Dinner was great. You were right about the picnic. It was a nice touch."

So the grouchy bear was offering a compliment. A pleased smile snuck across her lips. "I guess dinner voided your decision we stay away from one another."

"Yeah, well." His hand came up, rubbing the creases forming over his forehead. "I guess that was dumb of me to suggest, considering the circumstances."

They sat in an easy silence, both gazing into the wavering flames of the fire. Once the intense heat began to diminish, Hunter pushed up from his pillow and tossed another log inside the metal grate.

When he sat back down, he bypassed his pillow, settling at her side instead. His thigh brushed hers as he stretched his long legs in front of him. His broad shoulder rubbed against her side as he leaned back onto his arms.

This was how they'd gotten themselves into trouble the night before. Being close put a damper on their better judgment, leaving them helpless in the face of the desire brewing between them.

****

Hunter couldn't explain why he chose to sit so close they were touching. He could have easily sat back on his pillow. Or better yet, thanked her for the meal and retreated to another part of the cabin. The latter would have been his best choice.

Yet, here he was, back in the same predicament he'd sworn he was going to avoid. The rain pattered lightly against the windows while the fire gently warmed the air inside. The flames cast brilliant shadows over them as the soft crackling of wood filled the easy quiet.

"How long do you think we'll have to stay here?" Paxton's soft voice drifted in the peaceful air. With her chin resting on bent knees, she stared into the fire.

"I wish I knew. I gave my partner the name you supplied the other night. If we're lucky, your tip will pay off and the Bureau will finally get Grant behind bars where he belongs."

"What if they never catch him?" A trace of fear laced her words.

Instinctively, he swept a comforting arm around her shoulders. "They will. Someway, somehow, Grant is going down."

If his partner and the rest of the Bureau couldn't do it, he'd find a way to take down the man himself. When Paxton laid a trusting head against his shoulder, he knew he would make seizing Grant his own personal vendetta if he had to. There was no way he was going to let her live the rest of her life in fear.

"It gets so hard." Her warm breath brushed against his neck. "I can convince myself most of the time that I'm just on a little vacation, taking some time off from my regular life. But there are other times when I can't deny the truth. When I have to face the fact that somebody actually wants me dead, and I am literally running to save my life."

He cuddled her closer to his side, fitting her curves against him. He knew he was breaking his promises, shattering his resolve to keep a fair distance between them. But he couldn't turn away from her when she needed him to lean on. He would have comforted anyone in her situation.

The light scent of honeysuckle tickled his nose. Underneath, where his hand rested on her bare arm, he felt the silky softness of her skin. She felt so small, fragile, an image he never thought he'd place on a woman like her. But fright did strange things to people. He'd seen it many times in his career—levelheaded, calm victims losing all sense of sanity when they came to realize their lives were in danger.

He had to admit she was holding up pretty good considering the circumstances. There were times she let fear take over. But more often than not, she took everything with a steely spine and a stubborn tilt of her chin.

A laugh escaped Paxton. One holding no humor, only disbelief and irony mingled into one. "Who would believe this?" She shifted so she could look at him. With a single finger, he swiped a stray strand of hair from her forehead.

"Paxton Walsh, heir to the Walsh fortune, respected member of Denver's society, on the run from a crazed fiancé. Holed up in some remote cabin with an ex-lover. Just think what a heyday the gossip columns would have with this story if they ever learned the truth."

"I'd rather not," he grumbled.

Sapphire eyes met his, while a soft, sad smile played across Paxton's mouth. Unable to stop himself, he reached out, and rubbed the pad of his thumb against her bottom lip. "We're going to get you out of this mess. Before any of those gossip writers have a chance to learn the truth about anything."

Pushing up, she brushed a kiss across his mouth. "Thank you."

"For what?"

"For taking care of things. For protecting me from the idiot I was actually going to marry." Another smile graced her lips. "You know, even when you're acting like a jerk, you're still a pretty good guy."

He wasn't sure if he had just been given an insult or a compliment. In one sentence, she'd managed to call him a name and praise him at the same time. The name-calling he deserved, but the praise—that he couldn't accept until he got them out of this mess alive.

She inched closer, her eyes holding him captive. She obviously didn't expect a response. Her heavy lids and pouting lips asked for something else altogether.

What was it he'd sworn to earlier? For the life of him, he couldn't remember. The beauty in his arms clouded his thoughts. His common sense shattered when her soft body pressed seductively against his.

He felt the heat of her lips before they ever met his. She was slow, cautious, in seeking a kiss, her soft mouth brushing over his, waiting for his response. Her lips trembled as they connected with his. Questions sparkled in her eyes as she met his gaze.

Hell, he couldn't blame her for not knowing how

he'd react. He'd spent their time together turning from hot to cold in a blink of an eye. It only made sense she was reserved with her affection, afraid of being turned away again.

Well, it wasn't going to happen this time. His arms circled her, clasping at the curve of her back, pulling her close. He sought her mouth, leaving a trail of tiny kisses from one edge of her lips to the other. He traveled higher, including the tip of her nose and the rosiness of her cheeks.

She sighed, sinking into him with total abandonment. Her hands flattened against his chest, kneading the rigid muscles through the thin material of his shirt. He responded with another journey to her mouth. He deepened the kiss, urging her to open to him.

She did so easily while his hands splayed up her sides, gently massaging her. He wanted this. He couldn't deny it. Tomorrow, he'd deal with the consequences. Tomorrow, he'd let doubt and uncertainty settle in.

But tonight—

Tonight, he was going to let go, release all the reasons why he shouldn't be here, wrapped tight with Paxton. It had been too long of wanting this. Wanting to find that secret desire only she could give.

He growled in need, shifting his weight, easing her onto the blanket. Their legs knotted together while he shifted above her, running his hands through her hair. He held her face still. With wide eyes, she watched as he slowly lowered, claiming her lips as his own.

Her hips came off the floor to meet seductively with his. Firm, round breasts pushed against his hardened chest, giving him a feel of the rapid pounding of her heart. It beat a frantic rhythm, matching his own excited state.

Breaking the kiss, he hovered above, the muscles in his arms flexing with an effort to hold his weight up. "So beautiful." He leaned down and left a trail of kisses along the curve of her neck. "So very beautiful."

His mouth ventured lower, heating a path down the v-line of her shirt. She tasted sweet with temptation. The purr tumbling through her filled him with an even more urgent need. One hand came around to cup her breast while his mouth continued to work around the top line of her shirt, finding and relishing the creamy curve of her other breast.

She gasped as his fingers found her nipple through the shirt, giving a light tug on the hardened tip. She arched against him, her body begging. God, how he wanted her. Wanted this. He needed to feel her bare skin against his. Needed to be swallowed away in the sweetness of her warmth.

Her hands crept down his sides, pausing at the edge of his jeans. Warmth surged as she tugged the ends of his shirt free, splaying her fingers out across his bare back. Her head rose from the floor, finding the spot between his neck and ear. With a lavish kiss, she moved over his rough chin, trailing to the other side.

He locked his arms around her, switching their positions in one quick sweep. With his back on the floor, he gazed into her misty-eyed expression. Her knees rounded his sides. Her warmth settled over his hardness.

He took another kiss, delving deep into her mouth until she sighed with pleasure. His fingers curled around the bottom hem of her shirt, pushing it up her sides. She straightened, raising her hands in the air, helping to remove the barrier between them.

He knew this was it. There was no turning back. He eased the shirt over her breasts, baring the small mounds, covered in pink lace, to his greedy stare. At her shoulders, he tugged gently then paused, his senses on immediate alert.

His hands stalled as his ears tuned in to their surroundings. He listened, waiting for a sign of what had alerted him.

It came again and this time he had no doubt what it was. Somewhere outside, old twigs crunched under the weight of heavy, looming footsteps.

They weren't alone anymore.

Chapter Thirteen

"What?"

Hunter's sudden retreat left Paxton cold, confused. For a moment she'd been sure he was backing away again, leaving her desperate, wanting, as he had the night before.

But the probing look in his dark eyes and the harsh creasing of his brow told her something else was going on. Something she had no clue of.

He pressed a finger to her lips, shaking his head, discouraging any sound. With a quick yank, he had her shirt back down around her waist and then pulled her to her feet. His hand settled in hers, tugging her along at his side.

He paused at the corner of the couch, slinging his holster over his shoulder. Withdrawing his gun, he skirted them along the far wall of the cabin. "We have visitors. Stay behind me and don't utter a sound."

She nodded, flattening her back against the rough texture of the log wall. Her steps matched his as he led them around the outer edge of the room until they reached the front door. She hadn't heard or seen anything hinting they were no longer alone. But she trusted Hunter and didn't doubt someone had paid them an unwanted visit.

"Stand back." His hand rested on the door handle. "I need to make sure it's clear before we try getting out of here."

Again she nodded, fighting back the fear, praying for the horror to end.

Slowly, he eased the door open, his gun preceding him as he crept against the edge to peer out into the deep black night. Holding her breath, she waited while he searched the area between them and the Cherokee. Her hands shook. Fisting them, she stuffed them behind her back.

"Okay." He stepped back in the cabin far enough to hold out his hand. As soon as her palm rested in his, he tugged gently, plastering her tight to his side. "We have to move fast. Whoever is out there isn't going to wait much longer before making their move."

They slipped quietly into the threatening night. She tightened her hand around Hunter's as darkness settled. Moving them toward the Cherokee, his body was tense as he watched for signs of danger.

She saw the shadow of her car only a few steps ahead. They were going to make it. A relieved sigh escaped even as a large hand whipped out from the tree at her side, yanking her painfully from Hunter's grip.

A foul smelling black glove fell over her mouth, smothering the scream pushing from her lips. Something cold and round pressed against her temple as she was dragged back into what felt like a brick wall.

"My, my, look what we have here." She cringed in disgust at the voice of her unseen attacker. Raising wide eyes to Hunter, she found him standing firm, gun pointed at the anonymous form behind her.

"Let her go." Both hands curled around the handle of his gun. His finger pressed against the trigger, ready for action.

"I don't think you're in any position to be giving orders. I'm the one holding a gun to your little lady here."

Adding conviction to his words, the man behind her tightened his hold around her waist, pushing the edge of the gun deeper into her temple.

Fear unlike any she'd known seeped through her bones. She was going to die here in the middle of nowhere. All because she'd made a stupid mistake, agreeing to marry a man who'd lied to her and convinced her he was something he wasn't.

"You won't kill her," Hunter challenged, his hold on his gun never wavering. "There's no money in it for you if you don't deliver her to your boss alive."

"True. But that don't mean I can't shoot her somewhere else that won't inflict death, just cause a whole bunch of agony."

The gun moved away from her temple and pushed against her side, digging painfully into flesh. "Let's see," he snarled against her ear. "If I take a shot right about here, I should miss all the vital organs."

Panic seized her heart. Only the look of strength and belief Hunter offered kept her from falling apart at the stranger's feet. Though he talked with the man, he kept his attention on her, his face communicating he'd get them through this.

"Drop your gun," the man ordered. "Drop it, or my trigger finger will get very itchy."

It was a no win situation as far as she could see. Hunter couldn't possibly drop his gun. If he did, he'd resign them both to certain death. But if he didn't, she had no doubt the brute of a man behind her was going to follow through on his threat to release a bullet into her side.

"All right," Hunter conceded. "I'll put the gun down."

His eyes never left hers as he held one hand high in the air and crouched to place the gun on the ground at his feet. In them, she saw what the other man could not. Reading his intentions clearly, without him ever speaking a word, she waited until he made his move.

As his gun brushed against the hard ground, he gave a slight nod, meant only for her. Raising her foot, she brought it back against the man's shin with all her force.

He let out a loud yelp of pain as Hunter barreled at them. A shot rang through the air before Paxton was shoved away, Hunter's head making contact with the man's paunchy middle. Scrambling out of the way, she watched helplessly as the two rolled around in a violent struggle to overtake one another.

She cringed when Hunter's fist rose high and came down, landing squarely against the man's chin. The loud pop of knuckles cracking against bone echoed, followed by a harsh curse from their unwelcome guest.

She wanted to do something to help, but knew she would only end up in Hunter's way. Just the same, she grabbed hold of a large rock protruding from the ground, ready to level it against the man's skull if she had to.

Her actions were for nothing. Turning back to the struggle, she watched Hunter deliver one last blow. The wrestling match ended as the man's eye rolled back in his head, hands falling lifelessly to the ground.

Her eyes widened in shock. "Did you—"

She took a deep breath to chase away the trembling

in her voice. "Did you kill him?"

Pushing to his feet, Hunter shook his head. "I didn't kill him." He reached out and took her hand. "Just knocked him unconscious long enough for us to get away."

With a gentle tug, he led her to the Cherokee, their footsteps hurried along the rough ground. After he tucked them safely inside, he fired the engine to life, and turned down the long drive leading away from the cabin.

Paxton glanced at him and noticed a strange stain flowering over the shoulder of his shirt. Twisting around for a better look, a frightened gasp escaped.

"You're bleeding." She touched the discoloration spreading across the top of his shirt. He flinched and glanced down to take a look.

"Damn." He slammed an open palm against the steering wheel. "The bastard got me with that last shot of his."

"We have to get you to the hospital."

He shook his head. "It's only a flesh wound." He ripped the seams of his shirt with one hand while steering the Cherokee down the narrow road with the other.

He bared the injury, giving it a quick glance. "The bullet clipped the top of my shoulder, nothing more."

"Nothing more?" Her mouth gaped open in disbelief. "It's a gunshot wound. People die from such injuries."

"Not this kind they don't. Look, the blood is already slowing down. A hospital can't do any more than we can as soon as we have a first aid kit in our hands."

She opened her mouth to protest, but stalled when his expression suddenly hardened into cold anger. Following the line of his gaze, she caught sight of the dark figure planted in the middle of the road. The Cherokee was quickly gaining on him, but he showed no signs of getting out of the way.

"How could he get all the way down here before us?" Her eyes locked on the quickly approaching shape blocking the road.

"It's not our friend from earlier." He shook his head. "I was wondering why the guy didn't have a partner. These people usually work in pairs."

"Doesn't he realize he's about to be run over?"

"I don't know." He kept a critical eye on the man.

His features became more prominent as they gained on him. Slowly, that which had only been blurred shadows in the night began to take shape. Dressed in black, it was hard to see him clearly in the limited light. His legs were spread apart, arms held out in front of him, grasping something between his hands.

It only took a second to realize what the man was holding.

"Get down." Hunter's hand landed against her back, shoving her head between her legs seconds before gunfire exploded around them. Shards of glass rained down, embedding in her skin, and tangling in her hair.

His string of angry curses assured her he'd been missed by the tirade of bullets. She turned her head and saw him staring out of what was only seconds ago the front windshield.

"Stay down." He spared her a brief glance. "He emptied his chamber. If we're lucky we can get past him before he has a chance to reload."

"Is he still standing in the middle of the road?" Her heart beat hard against her ribs as a frantic pulse echoed inside her head.

"The idiot hasn't budged. If I have to, I'll run him over."

She waited, hating the feeling of not knowing what was going on. She expected to hear more gunshots or the heavy thud of the Cherokee running the gunman down.

Neither came. Unable to take the suspense, she eased up, peering over the dashboard. "Where is he?"

He tilted his head back. "Behind us. He ran for the trees at the last second. I guess he decided he valued his life more than he first thought."

Relieved, she pushed back into her seat. Hunter's hand closed over her arm, stopping her. "Don't get up yet. We aren't out of danger. Our friend is still behind us. And, if I'm guessing right, he'll have his gun reloaded any minute."

As if in response, the air again exploded with the biting blasts of gunshots. She slid back into her place, hearing the back window shatter.

"Hold on." Hunter slammed his foot on the accelerator. The sudden rush of speed tumbled her forward on the floor, her forehead bumping against the dashboard.

"You okay?"

She nodded though her body ached from her bumped forehead to the glass still buried in her skin. She couldn't very well complain when Hunter had a gunshot wound to deal with even as he was trying to get them away from sure death.

"You're safe now." He spared her a quick look.

"We've left our uninvited guests far behind."

Biting her bottom lip to silence a pain-filled groan, she pushed back into the passenger seat. A cold wind swept over her, reminding her they no longer had any protection from either the front or the back of the Cherokee. Both windshields were gone, leaving only the side windows to provide protection from the forces of weather.

At least it had stopped raining. She couldn't image how much worse it would be if they still had the storm to deal with.

"Where are we headed?" She pulled small shards of glass from her arms, grimacing with each one she yanked from her flesh.

"We need to get another mode of transportation and find somewhere to settle down for the night. The sooner we can dump the Cherokee, the less chance we'll have of being found."

She nodded, giving no thought to the fact she was about to lose her cherished vehicle. In the face of what had happened, the worth of such material things plummeted.

"Are you doing okay?" She took another peek at the wound along his shoulder. He was right, it had already stopped bleeding, giving her some assurance he wasn't going to perish from the injury.

"It hurts like hell," he admitted. "I think I have some shards of glass buried inside the wound."

She flinched in pain at the thought. His arms carried the same red marks as hers from where he'd pulled glass from his skin. His face was covered as well. She wondered how he could handle his injuries so calmly.

"At the next town, we'll find a way to get our hands on another vehicle. Until then, why don't you try and get some rest."

She didn't argue, though she knew there wasn't a chance she would get any rest. The events of the past hour were slowly catching up, putting a fierce reality on what she'd witnessed. The ugly images she'd collected would haunt her for the rest of her life.

****

By sheer luck, he located a car rental agency in the next town they came to. Hunter was surprised to find that a town without a single fast food restaurant found it necessary to have access to rental cars along its main street.

After taking the risk of using his credit card for the rental, he had Paxton climb in behind the wheel of the sedan and follow him in the now worthless Cherokee. Outside of town, he found a remote field, overcrowded with weeds and brush. Going as far as he dared, he left the vehicle buried in a pile of thistles almost as high as his neck. Together, he and Paxton cleared all contents out of the vehicle. Removing the license plates, they left it bared and abandoned.

He took over the wheel of their rented sedan, heading them off for a long drive in the quiet of the night. He wanted to get as far away from the ditched Cherokee as possible.

At his side, Paxton rode along in silence. He knew the night had taken its toll. He wanted nothing more than to pull over, gather her in his arms, and chase away the demons haunting her.

For the sake of their safety, though, he knew he couldn't. Comfort would have to come later, once they were secluded away in some anonymous hotel room.

During the early hours of morning, they stopped at a little place outside of Sheridan, Wyoming. Ahead of them on the interstate was the beginning of more mountain territory. He didn't want to risk the drive during the night. Morning light would give him an easier go at the steep, curving mountain passes.

Again Paxton waited in the car while he reserved a room. The hotel had a little more class than the last one they'd stayed at. It was a popular chain of small, inexpensive hotels, promising cleanliness and a continental breakfast.

"Take off your shirt. I'll look for a first aid kit," Paxton instructed once they settled inside their room. This time, there were two double beds, eliminating the need for them to sleep together as they'd been forced to do the last time.

Picking the bed farthest from the door, he settled on the edge, and pulled his shirt over his head, baring his wounded shoulder. With her back to him, she rummaged through the drawers of a dark wood dresser, providing a wonderful sight to occupy his thoughts while she conducted her search.

"Found it." She turned with an old metal box clutched in her hands. Though she looked him straight in the eye, he had a feeling she wasn't actually seeing him.

The sapphire depths of her eyes were clouded. Tight lines pulled along her forehead and stretched her lips into a thin line. When she sat the first aid kit down on the mattress beside him, her hands trembled.

He linked her fingers with his and gave them a little tug, pulling her attention to where he sat. "Why don't you get some rest? I'll take care of my shoulder."

She shook her head. "What I need right now is to keep busy. Tending to your wound will help get my mind off everything that happened."

He didn't argue, understanding the need to occupy her mind. With a soft kiss to the top of each hand, he released her, letting her get back to work.

The pounding in his shoulder had faded to a dull ache in the time they'd been on the road. Paxton dabbed softly with an alcohol-drenched cotton ball. Cleaning dried blood from his wound, she exposed the throbbing cut slicing through the top layer of his skin. It was deeper than he first thought and would have required stitches if they were visiting an emergency room. As it was, a simple bandaging would help him heal just fine.

Her hands shook, and her eyes clouded as she cleaned his wound, treating it with a healing ointment that was cool against his bare skin. She finished her job with a butterfly bandage securely fastened on both sides of his shoulder, effectively holding the gaping wound together.

"You handled that like a professional." He stood up from the bed to observe her handy work in the mirror. "I take it you've had some experience in bandaging up the injured."

"You'd be surprised what harm teenage boys can do when they're playing basketball on the blacktop. I'm always having to bandage cuts and scratches where I work. Those rough and tough boys turn into meek babies when they hurt themselves."

"Aren't they lucky they have you looking out for them," he returned, coming up behind her, wrapping his arms around her slender waist. She fell against his chest and rested her head against his uninjured shoulder.

Tension held her captive. He tightened his hold. "You need some sleep," he whispered softly in her ear.

"No." She shook her head. "If I lay down and close my eyes, I'll be haunted with images of what happened. I'm not exactly used to having my life threatened with a gun held to my head."

A slight shiver shook through her. Cupping his hands around her arms, he turned her until she faced him. Hollow, frightened eyes looked into his through a face as pale as a ghost.

He felt her terror as if it were his own. Each tremble shaking her body passed through his limbs as well. He would have given anything to erase the shadows etched deep beneath her fear. Would have given his own life to have protected her from the horror she suffered.

Wanting only to offer comfort, he bent his head to meet hers, lightly brushing his lips against hers. What he hadn't expected was her sudden and surprising reaction to his simple touch.

Her hands clasped around the nape of his neck, body pressing against his. She pushed his head back down, capturing him in a kiss that had absolutely nothing to do with the comfort he'd thought to offer and everything to do with the heated desire they'd found earlier.

Desperation radiated through her hold. She clutched him as if he were her only lifeline to sanity. Her lips fused with his as he opened his mouth, allowing her the entrance she demanded.

As he pulled away, he saw moisture gathering in her eyes, softening their rich color. Trapping her bottom lip under her nibbling teeth, her expression fell into a look of uncertainty.

"Make love to me." Her tender gaze stabbed straight through to his heart.

He didn't answer. Couldn't answer over the tightness constricting the muscles in his throat.

"Please."

With a hungry growl, he swept her back into his hold, his lips finding hers in answer to her request. He knew she held him in hopes of erasing the ugliness. Needed him for more than just release of sexual tension. He was her escape. The one solid thing she could cling to in her currently mixed up life.

He also knew he wouldn't deny her any of those things. Tonight, he'd offer her the stability and certainty she craved. In the morning he'd deal with the price he would pay for doing so.

Without breaking the kiss, he backed toward the bed. The top of his shins tapped against the edge of the mattress. Easing down, he brought her along, straddling his thighs.

As soon as they were settled, the kiss deepened until they became one with each other, connecting their souls, their hearts. The tips of her fingers played desperately over his bare chest, molding every curve and line of muscle. Her hands slipped over his shoulders and around the nape of his neck, pulling him deeper into the kiss.

She moaned in protest when he pulled away, leaving them gasping for air. "Hunter." She reached blindly to pull him back.

He held her tiny wrists in one hand. "I want to see you. I want to love every part of you there is to love."

"Please, Hunter." She molded her heated body against his. He could see in her eyes she didn't want to wait. Didn't want to waste a second. She yearned to find the connection they shared. Ached for the fulfillment they both knew they'd find.

Her urgency fueled his desire, filled him with a sense of need so great he was afraid he was going to lose it right then and there. Fumbling with the bottom edge of her shirt, he grasped it and tugged it over her head. He tossed it carelessly to the floor, his attention turning to the lace covered breasts, exposed for his touch.

He cupped each breast in the palm of his hands, encircling them in a gentle hold. She responded by arching into him, filling his hungry fingers with the soft mounds. Pushing aside the lace, he found a hardened nipple begging for his touch. Lowering his head, he ran his tongue around the dark circle, teasing it to a tighter point.

Her hands tangled in his hair, holding him while he lavished her with tiny kisses, gentle nips. Her hips ground against him, feeding the growing fire. He pushed the hardness behind his zipper against her, giving proof of how badly he wanted her.

Reaching behind her, he separated the clasp of her bra, slipped the straps down her arms, and let it dangle off the edge of his finger for a second before sending it to join her shirt. She writhed across his thighs, as he again found her tempting breasts with his lips and ravished them with all the urgent need building inside.

She made him ache with desire. The longing inside was strong, carrying the weight of ten years without this pleasure. He hadn't gone without sex during the years they were separated. He'd found his fair share when he needed a release.

But nothing ever compared to what he found when he was buried deep inside Paxton. Their unions had been mind shattering, as fierce and demanding as a raging storm. There was something between them he could never quite explain or find when with another.

Falling back onto the bed, he took her with him, bringing her down on top of him. Her lips came to his, branding them in another hot, searing kiss. His heart pounded against his ribs as his pulse raged through his ears.

Without breaking their connection, he rolled her onto her back, hovering above her. He left her mouth to trail his lips along the high bones of her cheek and down the curve of her stubborn chin. He traced the route from her neck to her collarbone, taking his time, exploring every part of her inviting body.

Capturing first one breast then the other, he gave each equal treatment with the slow winding of his tongue. He slid his hand down, inching over the hem of her shorts to cup her softness in his greedy palm.

She was so alive under his touch—so full of passion, desire. Pushing her body toward him, she gasped with pleasure as he eased his hand inside her shorts, gently stroking with the pad of his finger.

Her hands lifted, stroked down the curve of his shoulders and along the line of his spine. Grasping the edge of his jeans, she fumbled with the button and zipper in a frantic attempt to remove them. He moved her fingers aside and kicked his legs to shed his pants, and tossed the remainder of his clothes, before he finished stripping Paxton from hers.

He took pleasure in her naked body sprawled out underneath him. Pushing onto his elbows, he gazed down at her beauty, taking in every shapely curve.

She was perfect—sweet and supple in every way. She looked at him with need darkening her eyes, lips red and swollen from their kisses. Even with the resentment he'd carried through the years, he needed this moment. Needed this chance to reclaim what was once his even if it was for only a brief time.

"You are so beautiful." He dropped feathery kisses along the gentle curves of her breasts.

He moved lower, tracing his mouth along the lines of her stomach. Finding his way to her legs, he kissed the inside of each thigh, while his hands crept up to caress her pointed nipples. He teased her with quick, almost nonexistent kisses in her most sensitive spot and smiled when he heard the tiny sounds she made.

He deepened the next kiss, knowing the havoc he caused. She groaned, grounding her fingers into his uninjured shoulder. He continued his torture, wanting her wriggling beneath him until she could stand no more.

Her fingers shoved into his hair as her hips came flying high off the bed. She squirmed against his mouth, giving him even more access to the sensitive swell between her legs. Whimpers escaped, satisfying him to know he could still affect her as he once had.

"Please, Hunter," she pleaded in a raspy, deep tone. He glanced up, finding her head swinging against the pillow, bottom lip captured between her teeth.

After one more kiss, he slid up her body, pushing her legs farther apart with his knee settling between hers. He locked his lips with hers for a heat-filled moment before he rose above her, pushing against the edge of her welcoming warmth.

"Look at me, princess." Her lashes fluttered open, revealing the cloud of desire hidden behind them. He held her gaze, wanting to watch her reaction as he buried himself inside.

Biting down on every bit of control he held, he slowly entered, feeling her close around him as he slid deep inside. Pleasure so deep it doubled his own washed over her face. He growled in impatience, struggling to hold himself together. Her hips jumped underneath him as she closed her legs around him until nothing separated their bodies.

"Slowly, sweetheart." He kissed the tip of her nose. "Or this will be over before it ever gets started."

Giving him his request, she allowed him to set the pace, matching each thrust with a seductive swirl of her hips. Every muscle in his body grew taut along his back as he tried to stretch their lovemaking out, wanting it to never end.

It felt so right, as if he'd found a part of him that had been lost for so long. She made him feel as if he was on the top of the world, capable of anything.

Her hand crept between them, easing down to where they were joined. The second he felt her finger graze against him he knew all was lost. A sound of pure defeat escaped him as he pushed into her again and again, losing sense of everything but the woman beneath him.

She matched his every thrust, giving while she took. Her legs tightened around his waist, pulling him in even more. With a whimper, her eyes widened, her body tensed. He knew she clung to the edge of release.

"It's okay, sweetheart. Let it go."

Sapphire eyes met his, blazing with desire. Keeping the pace to their frantic lovemaking, he watched her tumble over the edge, giving into the burst of waves rocketing through her body.

Her release shuttering around him was all he needed to push him over the edge as well. Crying out her name, he stiffened. His world shattered as he collapsed on top of hers.

Time lost all meaning as he slowly slid back to reality, long, deep breaths helping slow the frantic beat of his heart. For a long moment, he did nothing but savor the union between them, closing his eyes, holding the images.

Beneath him, she shifted and he rolled on to his back. Pulling her with him, he cradled her into the crook of his arm. Her honey-blond hair spread over his chest as she snuggled into his side. With his free hand, he grabbed hold of the disheveled blankets and pulled them over their naked bodies.

Holding her tight, he slid into sleep with a small smile on his lips.

Chapter Fourteen

Paxton awoke buried in the crook of Hunter's arm. Stretching tired muscles, she glanced up and caught him staring at her through the early morning light peeking through the curtains.

"Good morning." He dropped a kiss on the tip of her nose.

"Mmm." She snuggled closer. "It most certainly is."

It felt so right waking up in his arms. I love him, she thought, knowing she didn't dare speak the words aloud. She'd always loved him. Always would. But the past stood in their way, forming a barrier that needed to be brought down.

His hand slid down her back, cupping her bare bottom. "We should be getting out of bed," he told her though he made no move to do so. "It's best to get on the road as soon as possible."

"Okay." She tossed her leg over his, wiggling against him. Her hand stroked the rigid lines of his chest as her fingers tangled in the dark hair there.

"Paxton."

Looking up, she plastered an innocent look across her face. "What?"

"We really should be getting up."

"I know. You already said that." With an evil smile, her hand slid down his chest. Her fingers slithered over his washboard stomach, sliding below the edge of the blanket around his waist. She clasped her hand around him, smiling when he moaned with pleasure.

He was right about having to go, but she didn't want to leave the tiny room yet. Not when the real world hovered outside the door. All she asked for was a little more time snuggled in bed where she could forget everything and think only of the way he made her feel.

"Paxton," he groaned as she stroked him. His rough hands rested on her shoulders, curling around them with a frantic grasp.

She was getting to him and loved every minute of it. It had been so long since she'd affected someone the way she did Hunter. With Grant, everything had been as organized and controlled as the rest of his life, leaving no room for chaos to enter even the privacy of the bedroom.

But with Hunter, it had never been that way. From their first night, when he'd taken her virginity, there were never rules when it came to their lovemaking. Emotions ruled, setting the frenzied tone every time they came together.

She loved bringing him to his knees, knowing what she did to him with no more than a single touch. It had fueled her desire as a lovesick teenager and continued to do so even as a grown, mature adult.

She bent over, placing a soft kiss along his swollen length. His responding groan rumbled through his body, encouraging her. There was pleasure for her by the simple act of satisfying Hunter. A wave of shivers raced up her spine and puckered her nipples in responding passion.

This was where she belonged. Where she had always belonged. Since the first moment he stepped into her life, he'd become the part that made her whole. Being with him, sharing the intimate moments of two lovers, made her feel safe, secure, happy. Even their current danger faded to a pale threat when she was held in the fold of his arms.

A sexy smile grew across her lips as she ravished him in the same way he'd done to her the night before. She teased, tempted, and stroked the fire until it burned out of control.

A low, painful sound rose through him seconds before he tugged on her arms, stretching her over him. "I need to be inside you."

Large hands circled her tiny waist, lifting her up for a fraction of a second before slowly lowering her. He filled her in one swift motion causing her breath to catch in her chest. Her head fell back in complete abandonment.

At first neither of them moved. Just being connected in the most physically intimate way created pleasure, bringing them together in much more emotional ways.

Finally, she shifted over him, using her own feminine wiles to tease with every stroke. Her palms flattened against his chest as her gaze clashed with his. She took her time, drawing out each minute into pure torture. Even as he tried to quicken the pace, she stopped him, moving with a precise beat, stroking the embers into a slow burning inferno.

Tension spiraled through her limbs, building tighter and tighter. There wasn't a place on her body that didn't tingle with awareness as excitement coiled inside. Higher and higher she climbed until she could take no more and the world began to spin.

Calling out his name, she shivered with the force of her release. Beneath her, he tightened, letting go at the same time, bringing them to tumble from their highest peaks together. Collapsing on top of him, she let the beat of his heart slowly ease her back to reality.

****

"You shower while I make a phone call," Hunter told her half an hour later when they finally rolled out of bed.

Paxton stood over the mattress, looking down at the crumpled sheets. The bed looked totally and completely broken in, evidence to what they'd shared. The thought sent another shiver of excitement up her spine, making her want for things she knew they no longer had time for.

For the first time since the whole crazy adventure began, she secretly hoped that it didn't come to a quick end. When the danger was over and her life was once again her own, she didn't want to think of what would happen between them. At least while she needed his protection she could count on other nights like the one they'd just shared.

Hunter left a kiss on her cheek and steered her toward the bathroom. Before she had the door closed, he'd settled in the only chair in the room, phone held to his ear.

The hot water felt good, slicing over muscles aching from a vigorous night of exercise. Since the necessities she and Hunter had bought were stuck back up at the cabin, she had to make do with the travel size shampoo and soap the hotel provided.

Scrubbed clean, she wrapped a thin white towel around her. Hitching it below her arms, she sauntered back into the room. With her first step out of the bathroom, she sensed the charged air replacing the earlier calm.

Hunter sat where she'd left him, back facing her as he stared out the window. The telephone was nestled between his ear and shoulder. His low, booming voice reached back to where she stood. Shoulders tense, his back was stiff and rigid. Whatever his conversation was, it wasn't doing much good for his mood.

"I don't have the faintest idea how they figured out where we were." He ran an aggravated hand through his sleep-tousled hair. "I took extra precautions to make sure I told no one of our destination. There should have been no way for Grant to have been tipped off to our whereabouts."

She stepped further into the room while Hunter paused for whatever was being said on the other end. He was unaware of her. She took the opportunity to listen to his conversation without his knowledge.

"We went into town once. And only long enough to pick up some food for the cabin. I'm positive she wasn't recognized, but can't think of any other way they would have learned of the cabin. Maybe somebody spotted her while we were in town and somehow the information got back to Grant."

The more he fumed, the larger the hole in the pit of her stomach grew. She had a feeling she knew how Grant had figured out where they were. Hunter may have been careful not to leak their destination, but she hadn't used the same caution.

Her hand flew to her mouth, silencing the gasp of

realization before he heard it. It was her fault they were found. She'd been the one to tell her father their general location. Obviously, he hadn't listened when she'd begged him not to tell Grant.

"Damn." His sudden curse rocked through the room. "It's my fault. I should have never taken for granted that we were safe. I should have known better. I've been on this job too damn long not to know to always expect the unexpected. My carelessness could have very well cost Paxton her life."

He was blaming himself. She shook her head back and forth, denying the guilt he crudely placed on his shoulders. She couldn't let him believe he was the one to blame. She deserved to carry the guilt, not Hunter.

She had to tell him the truth. She knew it. It was just a problem of getting up enough nerve to do so. He wasn't going to take such information with a smile and a shrug.

"Keep me posted." Ending the call, he turned and noticed her standing behind him. "You okay?"

She nodded. "Of course I am. Why would you ask?"

"You looked pretty pale there for a second."

Shrugging off his worries, she stepped away, unable to bear his closeness with the guilt riding around inside. "I'm fine."

He gave her one last searching look before moving away. "I'll shower then we can head out."

He strolled to the bathroom she'd vacated. "Don't answer the door to anyone." He disappeared inside.

With him gone, she collapsed onto the bed, hitching her elbows on her legs, burying her face in her hands. Last night she hadn't even thought of how those two thugs had found them. It was enough for her to digest they were there, wagging their guns all over the place.

Hunter had given it thought though, took it as his mistake they'd been found. Guilt weighed heavy on his shoulders.

There was no getting around telling him. She couldn't let him walk around thinking he hadn't performed his job in protecting her. He'd done everything he was capable of to keep her safe, saving her life more than once. There was no way she was going to let her fatal mistake become his.

With the hum of the shower droning in the background, she rehearsed a number of different ways to tell him. She played out every scenario inside her head, trying to find the right one that wouldn't cause his temper to flare.

By the time his shower ended and he reappeared in the room, she still had no idea of how she was going to tell him the truth of what she'd done.

****

Fifteen minutes under the searing spray of the shower hadn't worked the way he'd hoped. When Hunter stepped back into the room where Paxton waited, his body responded to the sight of her. Their night of lovemaking had only strengthened his long buried desire. No matter what he tried, he was unable to sweep it away as he'd been able to do in the past.

"Ready to go?"

He received a small nod. She stood in the center of the room, fingers laced together, face tight with an emotion he couldn't describe.

Maybe she was having the same doubts and

concerns he'd experienced since waking up with her in his arms. He couldn't call their lovemaking a mistake. Couldn't honestly say he regretted what happened. Being with Paxton had been everything, and more, than he remembered it to be.

But what happened still changed nothing between them. Just as before, they had no future. Of that, he was sure. He may have been foolish at twenty-one, believing they could overcome their differences. But with age, that foolishness was no more. He knew better than to start believing in happily ever after.

"We can stop and get something for breakfast once we get back on the road," he told her while they settled into the rental car. She sat quiet beside him, her attention diverted out the side window, hands knotted in her lap.

Silence filled the tiny space inside the car as he kicked up speed on the highway. He stopped only once, grabbing donuts and coffee before settling into the long drive taking them further away from the hunting cabin.

He wasn't sure where they were headed or what their next step should be. All he knew was that someway, somehow, they'd been discovered at the cabin which meant he could no longer consider any place safe.

Time was running out. The more missed attempts, the angrier Grant was sure to grow. He wanted Paxton. His desperation had to be mounting with each day that passed without getting what he wanted. He'd already killed once to stay out of jail. He would do it again.

"Where are we going?" Paxton's quiet voice broke through his thoughts.

"I don't really know." He spared her a glance. "I

want to keep us moving as long as possible. If Grant was able to find us before, he can find us again. I don't plan on giving him many more opportunities to do so. We're safer when we're on the move."

"I overheard you talking on the telephone earlier." She looked at him, her sapphire eyes burning into his side. "Are they going up to the cabin to look for the two who came after us?"

"They'll go up there, but they won't find anything. Those two are long gone. I doubt they were careless enough to leave anything behind."

"I'm sorry they found us."

"Yeah. Me too." He was surprised at what he found when he looked at her. Her bottom lip was trapped beneath her teeth and worry lines creased the delicate skin around her eyes. The nightmare was taking its toll. It was all he could do not to reach out and place a comforting hand on her trembling leg.

"No, Hunter." She shook her head. "I mean, I'm telling you that I'm sorry they found us."

"Why would you do that? You had no control over what happened."

She turned back to the window but not before he caught the dark expression clouding her face. "But I think I did," she admitted so quietly he strained to hear her over the gentle rumble of the engine. "I think I'm the reason they knew where to find us."

His fingers tightened around the steering wheel. "Why do you think that?" He was sure he was going to dread the answer.

"Because, when I talked to my father, I gave him the general idea of where we were. They must have figured it out from there."

"When exactly did you talk to your father? How was it that I knew nothing about it?" He fought to keep his growing frustration under control.

"You didn't know, because I didn't tell you." She looked at him only a moment before turning away. "That day we went into town, I called my father from the store to let him know I was okay."

Damn. He smacked his hand against the steering wheel. He'd known she was up to something, hiding some truth from him. He'd made a promise to find out what it was, but he'd been distracted by other things and never questioned her. If he had, he would have expected their visitors.

"Why the hell would you do such a thing?" Losing control, his anger surged. He was mad but not just at Paxton. He was mad at himself and the error he made in not pushing for information when he should have. It was a critical mistake people in his line of work couldn't afford to make. He knew better. His foul-up could have cost them both their lives.

"I didn't think there was any harm in letting my dad know I was okay." Her voice turned defensive. "I didn't want him to worry about me. And I was afraid of what Grant might be telling him."

"So you decided to go behind my back and call him." He shook his head, frustrated. "Not only that, you go and tell him where to find us."

"He insisted I tell him. I asked him not to tell Grant."

"And you believed he wouldn't go running to your fiancé as soon as he heard from you? Come on, Paxton, we both know your father better than that. He probably called Grant the second you told him goodbye."

A spark of defiance dashed through her eyes. She crossed her arms defensively over her chest. "What did you expect me to do, let my father worry about what happened to me?"

"No. I expected you to tell me you wanted to let him know you were okay rather than going behind my back."

"You never would have let me call him."

"You're right. I wouldn't have," he agreed through clenched teeth. He swerved the car to the far left lane, avoiding a slow moving truck then turned to Paxton. "But I would have arranged for somebody to get word to your father that you were okay. If you would have come to me, I would have made sure somebody from the Bureau contacted him and let him know not to worry."

"And how was I supposed to know you would do that?"

His temper seethed, anger burning straight through to his toes. When was she going to stop answering to Daddy Dear? Behind his back, she'd called him and given their safe haven away.

Of course, he would go straight to Grant with her whereabouts. It wouldn't have mattered to him that his own daughter had asked him not to. In the eyes of Theodore Walsh, Grant was perfect husband material. He'd stop at nothing to make sure their wedding turned out successful, regardless of his daughter's wishes.

"You could have trusted me enough to know I would have understood your concerns and would have done whatever I could to take care of them."

He didn't move when her gaze stroked his side. "Like a fool, I believed we had some semblance of trust. Obviously, I was mistaken. It's just like ten years ago, isn't it? I seem to see the relationship between us in a completely different light than you. I should have known better."

"And I should have known better than to think you might actually understand that I made a mistake, and I'm sorry for it."

Tension crackled between them, taking them back to the same footing they'd tread upon after he'd kidnapped her from her wedding. The silent truce they'd come to had flown out the window, lost in the angry words tossed between them.

It was better this way. He was getting way too comfortable having her around. This was what he needed—a reminder to stick to his job and forget about the beauty of the woman at his side.

Nothing had changed between them, though he'd begun to believe otherwise. She was still a daddy's girl and he was still fighting through the problems it created. Theodore Walsh had made his life miserable during the months he'd dated his daughter. Even now, though he was doing his best to keep his daughter safe, he still had his hand stuffed in the middle, bringing about more problems where they were needed the least.

Chapter Fifteen

They were just outside Bozeman, Montana when Hunter stopped in front of a quaint, country home settled on the banks of a small lake.

"What are we doing here?" They were the first words Paxton dared since their argument.

It was for the best. She didn't figure they had anything nice to say to one another. Trying to talk would have only fed the tension warring between them.

"We're checking in for the night." Hunter turned off the car and pushed open his door.

"Here?" She strained her neck from side to side, taking in the scenery. It was a peaceful valley, alive with the sounds and sights of summer. A group of ducks swam lazily through the still lake water, enjoying the shade of towering pines at its side. Flowers of every kind and color stretched the length of the house, showing many hours of love and attention.

Stepping out from her side, she pulled fresh air into her lungs as a soft breeze rustled the ground at her feet. The summer sun settled in the western sky, shooting a blaze of orange and red across the mountaintops.

"It's a bed and breakfast." Hunter came around the front bumper to join her. "I thought we'd be safer here than at another small motel off the highway. This place is so well hidden, you have to know about it in order to find it."

"So I take it this isn't your first visit." She hoped her voice didn't reveal the sudden streak of jealousy that shot through her. The place centered on love and romance. From the house to the delicate setting surrounding it, it had to be a favorite among lovers.

She didn't want to think of him coming here with another woman.

"No, it's not." He stepped in front of her, leading the way inside. He held the door for her then turned toward the cozy reception area off to the right.

She stopped in her tracks as a large, burly sort of man stood up from a leather recliner. He didn't fit into her portrait of this little romantic getaway. What she expected was a soft, elderly woman with love-struck eyes and a charming smile. What she got was a man who looked as weathered as old leather and hard enough to bite nails with his teeth.

"Well, well, Reese. It's about time you came back for a visit." He stuck a thick hand out. "And this time you actually brought a woman along. I'm impressed."

Crystal blue eyes lit mischievously as the man graced Paxton with a crooked smile, deepening the aging lines across his face. "Names Ashland Gray." He offered the same hand he'd given Hunter. "And this here is my little getaway on the lake."

"It's beautiful." She smiled, as intrigued by Ashland as she was by his bed and breakfast. "It must be very popular with honeymooners."

"Honeymooners, married couples." He waved his hands in the air. "We get all kinds here. Had myself a couple a few months ago who had dated in high school fifty years back. They hadn't seen each other since graduation and it was here they chose to come for their reunion."

"How romantic." A breathless air drifted through her voice. Even in the front room, the magic of the place was clear. A small fire crackled in a fireplace tucked discreetly in the corner. A crystal chandelier offered muted lighting from above. The smell of honey and jasmine danced in the air, a soft scent that tickled the nose.

"So, tell me, how did you get so lucky as to finally snag this man?" Ashland tossed a heavy arm around her shoulders, leaning close for an answer. "I've been telling him for years that the purpose of this place was to bring along a woman, but he kept coming alone. It's good to see he finally followed through on my advice."

"Don't be getting any ideas, Gray," Hunter cut in before she had a chance to answer. "This isn't a romantic getaway. I was hoping you could tuck us away for the night. There are a few unsavory fellows looking for us. I don't want to be caught on the road when night hits around these parts."

Ashland tossed her a knowing smile before leaving her side to step behind the large, oak desk, sprawled along the far wall. Reaching below the desk, he brought forth a simple silver key, holding it out in his open palm. "Give you the best room I got."

"That's not necessary." Hunter shook his head. Paxton watched as he stepped up to the desk, a sinking feeling in her gut. Her confession that morning had taken care of what they'd shared the night before. While her spirits lifted with the thought of receiving the best room in this romantic little place, Hunter wasn't so happy about it.

"Don't you go telling me what is necessary in my

own place." Ashland waved the key at him. "You take this room or no room."

He was about to argue further, but after a stubborn look from Ashland, Hunter gave in, accepting the key as it dropped into his hand. Listening to the directions of how to find their room, he hooked a hand around her elbow and led her in the right direction.

"Interesting friend of yours." They moved down a long hallway to a set of curving stairs tucked away in the back corner of the house. "He sure doesn't strike me as the type to be running a cozy little bed and breakfast."

"He's only owned this place for a little over three years. It was falling apart when he first bought it. He's put in a lot of time to turning it around, making it into what you see today."

Side by side, they climbed the stairs, the thick gray carpet muffling their footsteps. "So how is it that you two know each other?"

"Ashland used to be an agent with the Bureau. A darn good one, too. His work in figuring out the demented minds of serial killers has helped solve more than one tough case."

She paused in surprise at the top of the stairs. "That man used to work with serial killers and now he's in charge of this little romantic getaway? I can't believe that."

Hunter shrugged, urging her forward. "He wasn't ready to lie around all day when his retirement came up. He decided to buy this place to keep busy. It's been good for him."

They stopped at another landing, there were only three more steps leading up to a set of oak double doors. He wrestled the key into the lock, then threw the doors open, and stepped aside so she could enter.

What she saw inside took her breath away. When Ashland claimed he was giving them the best room he had, he hadn't been lying. It was more of a suite than a room, tucked away in a small alcove in the back corner of the house. Windows circled the room on three sides, giving a beautiful view of the swaying trees just beyond their reach.

The colors, pale peach and ivory white, offered a soft tone of romance. It smelled of apples and spice, reminding her of homemade pies baking in the oven.

"It's beautiful." She couldn't stop the breathless comment as she stepped further into the room. Hunter followed, locking the doors behind him.

In the center of the room sat a large feather bed overflowing with fluffy white pillows tossed carelessly over the top. A thick peach comforter edged in delicate lace brushed the plush peach carpet she couldn't wait to sink her bare feet into.

"Sure puts those other motel rooms to shame." He pushed passed, moving from one window to the other before turning back to the center of the room. "We should be safe here. At least for tonight."

She nodded. She didn't want to be reminded of the danger waiting for them outside the door. Hidden away inside this romantic room, she could almost forget about Grant, his thugs, and the days they'd spent running for their lives.

Locked behind the doors, she could pretend everything in her life was perfect. Pretend she and Hunter had come here because they wanted to. Because they'd chosen to rekindle the love they once shared.

"Ashland should be sending dinner up soon." He kicked off his shoes, sinking onto the corner of the bed. "We can eat then get some rest before setting back out again tomorrow."

How could he be so immune to their surroundings? Here she was with crazy romantic dreams filling her head while all he thought about was their next escape plan.

She really had blown any chance between them. He obviously didn't intend to repeat what had happened the night before.

It didn't mean she had to go along with his intentions or lack of them. Kicking off her own shoes, she padded across the room. Peeking inside the bathroom, she found a large Jacuzzi tub just begging to be used. Along the sides of the tub, two rose shaped crystal holders held long, peach candles with new wicks sticking from their tops.

She'd regret it for the rest of her life if she didn't at least take advantage of the circumstances placing her and Hunter in a place like this.

"Let's start a fire." She turned away from the bathroom. Her feet sank in the thick carpet as she crossed to the dark stone fireplace across from the feather bed.

"There's no need." He shook his head. "This room will have no problem maintaining its warmth through the night."

"I don't want a fire for warmth." Bending on her knees, she tossed one log after another into the empty hearth. "This room doesn't feel complete without a fire burning. It's like the missing element in the whole decor."

"Suit yourself." He shrugged. Falling back onto the mattress, he stretched out his long limbs while she struggled to retrieve a match from the tiny box at her side.

Starting a fire didn't prove as easy as she first believed. She figured she could handle it after days of watching Hunter do the same. But where he made it look effortless, she found she couldn't get a spark to light no matter how hard she tried. She began to wish for the switch in her own place where one flick and the fire was roaring.

"You're doing it wrong." His voice sounded closer than before. Glancing over her shoulder, she noticed he'd pushed back to a sitting position. Seated on the corner of the bed, he was only a few feet away.

Ignoring him, she turned back to her task, growling in frustration as she tossed yet another burned out match onto the pile of logs.

The warmth of his body suddenly surrounded her. Her nerves pricked with awareness as his clean, musky scent filled her nose.

"Here, let me." He held his hand out for the matches.

Knowing it was foolish to argue when she was failing in getting the fire started, she handed them over and scooted out of his way.

He stepped up and rearranged the logs, adding smaller pieces of wood she hadn't seen. In a fraction of the time she'd spent in front of the fireplace, he had the logs lit, stoking the orange-red flames into obedience.

A small knock on the door echoed through the room as he straightened his long legs. She pushed up from the floor while he answered the knock, standing aside while a young girl hurried in, pushing a long white cart.

"Ashland said to serve your dinner in your room." She stopped at the small table and placed tray after tray along the surface.

Paxton's eyes grew large, watching and wondering what delights were hidden underneath the trays. It looked like Ashland planned to feed a small army rather than just two people.

When she finished, Hunter followed her and slipped a twenty-dollar bill into her hand before closing the doors behind her.

"Let's eat." He moved to the table, withdrawing one lid after another.

"Hold on." She bypassed the table, ignoring his curious glance. Moving quickly, she lowered the lights in the room. Ducking into the bathroom, she grabbed the crystal candleholders.

Fumbling with the knobs on the radio, she settled on a soft rock station before lighting the candles, and then settled down at the table.

"It's just food, Paxton." He pushed a plate of prime rib at her, snagged the other one for himself. "I don't think we need to make such a big affair out of it."

"Speak for yourself." Uncovering one of the trays, she found baked potatoes and fresh crispy rolls. Grabbing one of each, she dropped them onto the plate with her prime rib. Still there was more—a tossed salad, popcorn shrimp, along with a serving bowl of small red potatoes and baby peas together in a sinfully thick cheese sauce.

"This must be for dessert." Miniature sized cheesecakes covered the last tray with fresh strawberries dripping off their sides.

"I forgot to mention, Ashland loves to cook. It's always been his favorite pastime." Hunter sank his teeth into his first bite of prime rib, his eyes rolling with delight. "The guy used to bring homemade cookies and brownies with him to the office. We knew whenever he was working on a particularly hard case we could expect him to feed everyone in the department."

"Mmm," she responded around her first bite of meat. "Remind me to compliment the chef when we see him again."

After that, there was no reason for words. The food was too good to waste time talking. After what they had been eating over the course of the past week, the meal was heaven. She planned on enjoying every last bite.

The logs crackled with heat and cast shadows over the room. Moonlight streamed through the small gap in the curtains. A slow love song picked up on the radio while the flames of the candles danced over them.

She smiled, satisfied with the romantic mood she'd created. With each bite, she felt Hunter relaxing more and more. The hard creases lining his expression eased, erasing the tension he'd carried through the day. Shoulders that had been stiff and uncompromising only an hour ago, rolled back in comfort.

By the time he'd finished his meal, he was looking across the table with a more curious than angry spark in his dark gray eyes. "I should still be mad at you." He tossed the last bite of cheesecake into his mouth.

She nodded with a sly smile. "But you're not."

"I was. But I guess I'm just a forgiving sort of person."

She wanted to ask if he was willing to forgive

everything between them but bit down on her lip instead. She'd succeeded in softening him up after his grueling behavior. The last thing she wanted was to risk putting him back into his foul mood.

They cleaned up their dinner mess, placing the cart littered with dirty dishes outside the door. Hunter pulled out a bottle of wine from the well-stocked mini bar she'd failed to notice earlier, offering her a glass of Chardonnay as they settled down in front of the fire.

Another slow love song poured from the speakers. "Would you care to dance?" He set his wine down on the table and offered his hand.

"Here?" She folded her hand into his, allowing him to help her up.

"Yes, here." He pulled her close. Wrapping his long arms around her waist, he tugged her against him. Swaying gently to the music, he led her in perfect step.

The warmth of the fire wrapped around them. She cuddled her head into his shoulders. They moved in perfect rhythm, never missing a step. Their bodies melded as one as he twirled them slowly around the room.

She missed this, missed being so in tune with him, aware of his every move. This was why she'd felt so incomplete for so long. It didn't have a thing to do with trying to get her own life in order. It had to do with Hunter. Being separated from him brought a huge rift to her soul and left her feeling like she was missing a vital part of herself.

With him back and his arms wrapped around her, she felt complete for the first time in years. This was where she belonged. Where she'd always belonged. Ten years ago, she had willingly given her heart to him and he still had his claim on it. She loved him. There would never be any denying it.

After Hunter came into her life, she hadn't dreamt of the charity balls and fancy dinners girls in her standing eventually became a part of. She'd dreamed of other things. Of a dark, handsome man who could make her heart soar. A life full of excitement and challenge. She'd sworn she'd never succumb to the boring ways of other society ladies. Would never give in to the day-to-day tasks of tennis lessons, fund raising events, gallery showings.

Yet, ten years later, she'd been ready to marry Grant and fall into the path she'd shied away from. She'd even considered, on Grant's request, giving up her work with the inner city kids so she'd have more time to be the perfect wife.

When the music drifted to an end, Hunter settled them back in front of the fireplace. Glancing up at him, she realized he'd saved her from much more than Grant's dangerous secrets. He'd rescued her from a life full of boredom and predictability. A life she'd never truly wanted.

She clasped her hands around the nape of his neck and pulled him down for a kiss, expressing every ounce of gratitude she held inside. With her lips, she told him of her love, the feelings threatening to burst.

She wanted to tell him in more ways, but a kiss would have to do. Before she could confess her never dying love, she had to tell him the truth about what had happened ten years ago. Had to let him know she hadn't stopped loving him and never wanted them to go their separate ways.

She had to tell him, but now wasn't the time. The

heated look clouding his gray eyes hinted he had other things on his mind.

He didn't say a word, only cradled her face in his hands. His eyes spoke for him, mirroring the passion she felt welling up inside. For a moment, neither uttered a word as time passed unnoticed. Hunter's dark eyes gazed into hers, caressing her with a simple look.

Slowly, so very slowly, he lowered his mouth, his gentle lips taking possession of hers in a long, drawn out kiss, deepening with each passing second. His fingers strayed upwards, twisting in her long hair. The heat of his body pressed into her, molding hardness to softness.

She sighed, falling into him with abandonment, placing her heart and soul in his hands.

Scooping her into his arms, he was careful not to break the kiss, moving them over to the welcoming bed. Softly, he lowered her to the mattress, pushing her hands away as she reached to pull off her shirt.

"Let me." Curling his fingers around the bottom hem, he carefully lifted it over her shoulders, his eyes flashing hungrily at the pale skin he exposed. His hands curled around her waist as he bent down, leaving butterfly kisses across the smoothness of her stomach.

She pushed to the edge of the bed and curled her fingers over Hunter's broad shoulders, watching his dark hair brush softly against her pale skin. His hands circled her back, caressing up her spine until he found the latch to her bra. Releasing the two small hooks, he freed her breasts to his eager mouth.

She let her head fall back with a gasp as his lips circled one rosy nipple, teasing until it tightened with desire. He cupped the other with his palm, the pad of his thumb brushing against the already hardened nipple.

He brought a slow, sweet torture, as his hands and mouth caressed every inch of bared skin. He teased her hardened nipples until she whimpered for mercy, unable to take a second more. Her whole body ached with need so deep it pulsated through her veins.

Using the weight of his body, he eased her down, flattening her back against the soft mattress. In seconds, he had her completely bared to his hungry eyes. He stepped back and gazed at her, making love to her naked body with only the heat of his passionate stare.

She didn't move. She lay before him, exposed in the most intimate of ways. Her breasts were full, pointed with desire. Hunter's heated gaze swept between her thighs, resting on the tiny triangle of blond curls.

He knelt on the floor beside the bed and cupped her gently between her legs. "You're ready for me." He left a trail of kisses from her ankle to the curve of her knee as his fingers slipped inside her.

His kisses moved higher until he eased around the curve of her thigh, fingers stroking her closer to the edge.

"Please, Hunter," she begged as he found her heated core. Her hips rose off the mattress, pushing into him. With his hands curled around her waist, he held her close, exploring until she cried out, begging for him.

She couldn't take anymore. Pushing into a sitting position, she clenched her hands around his shoulders, holding him away.

He remained kneeling on the floor. She wrapped her legs around his sides, crossed her ankles behind him, and urged his body into hers. The proof of his desire pushed against the dampness between her legs. His mouth claimed hers, crushing her lips under the force of his need. Grinding her hips against him, she opened, and he buried himself inside with one hard thrust.

For a moment, neither moved as the intensity of their joining swept over them. He pushed deep. She gasped from the fullness stretching her. What started slow and gentle in front of the fire turned into a frantic need pulsating between them.

Over and over again they met, hearts pounding desperately together, bodies coated in dampness clinging to barc skin. She was close to tumbling over the edge, but held on, waiting until the first shiver rocked his body. Letting go, she joined him in a release so intense, so strong their passionate cries filled the room.

****

It was a long while before Hunter's breathing evened out and his heart stopped pounding inside his chest. Stretched on his side with Paxton's supple body tucked against him, a slow, lazy smile formed. It had never been that way between them before. The intensity, the urgency fueling their lovemaking was unlike anything he'd ever known.

They'd always possessed something special when their bodies met. But tonight was almost frightening. His desperation to have her, become one with her, had overwhelmed him, crashing painfully when his needs were finally satisfied.

He tightened his arms around her as his gaze strayed to the darkness peering through the window.

He'd lived ten years without Paxton, had created a life for himself. And now, he wondered how he ever survived without her. Wondered how he was going to make it when they again went their separate ways.

He was a fool for getting involved again. A fool to let his heart open up to the woman who had shattered it so long ago. But he couldn't stop the emotions surfacing whenever she was in his arms. He'd been helpless against them a decade ago. He was just as helpless now.

"Hunter." Her soft voice broke through his muddled thoughts. Twisting in his arms, she came face to face with him. Rising up, she balanced the weight of her head on one arm so she could look directly into his eyes.

With a gentle finger, he wiped away a stray curl from her cheek. Moonlight peeked in through the window, silhouetting her in a soft light. Enhancing her beauty and teasing his urges all over again.

"Ready for round two?" Though he teased, his body tightened in anticipation.

She shook her head, a cautious expression falling over her. "First there's something I think you should know."

He tensed. He had a feeling he didn't want to hear what she was about to say. Toying with the idea of kissing her into silence, he figured she'd only persist once the kiss was broken. She had a look of determination warning against any sort of distraction.

Reluctantly, she pushed out of his arms, resting against the headboard of the bed. Bringing her knees to her chest, she tucked her arms around them, diverting her attention away.

"There's something I have to tell you." Doubt and uncertainty mixed painfully in her voice. "Something I should have told you a long time ago."

Feeling at a disadvantage, he pushed up from the bed, settled a few inches away from her tempting body. He wanted to reach out and stroke the skin bared to his gaze. But he sensed her need for distance, physically and emotionally.

"I lied to you." She refused to meet his gaze. "Ten years ago, when I told you I didn't love you, that I wanted something more out of my life, it wasn't the truth. I was telling you what I had to, not what I wanted to."

With the mention of their past, he stiffened. He didn't want to talk about it. There was no need to bring up old hurts. "That was a long time ago. Whatever happened back then hardly makes a difference now."

She faced him, sapphire eyes brimming with unshed tears. "But it does make a difference. It makes a big difference. I've just now come to realize what happened so long ago has never truly gone away. I've lived with that dark shadow over my head for years. It's time you knew the truth."

"I've never stopped loving you." She turned away again. "I wanted to spend my life with you. I used to believe we were destined to be together. As if the fates had directed our paths to cross from the very beginning."

"Well…fate can be cruel." He pushed up from the bed, rummaged around on the floor for his jeans. Jerking them up his legs, he moved away, unable to stay idle with the memories she tossed between them.

"I had to break things off with you." She watched

him, her face shadowed with doubt. "I had no choice."

"Everyone has a choice, Paxton."

Shaking her head, she sent pleading eyes in his direction. "At the time, I didn't think I did. My father threatened terrible things if I didn't stay away from you. Things I knew I couldn't stop him from doing."

Crossing back over to the bed, he settled on the edge of the mattress. "What kind of things?" He held her gaze with his own.

"He was going to make sure you had no future. You would have lost your student loan, your job, and maybe even your freedom. He was going to use every connection he had to make sure we had no future together."

Anger, as fresh and new as it had been years ago, surged through him, and he bolted up from the bed.

"I'm so sorry," she cried as he paced in front of her. "I didn't know what else to do. He was threatening to go to the police, have you arrested. I knew you'd never get into law enforcement if you had any sort of record."

"There wasn't anything he could have had me arrested for. We were both of age back then. There weren't any laws broken."

"I know that now. But I didn't then. All I knew was he was threatening to take everything away from you. If I didn't convince you to stay away, your life would have been ruined because of me."

"Not because of you." He fought back the worst of the anger, knowing it would do no good. "Because of your father."

She looked unconvinced. In her mind, it was her fault her father threatened to destroy his future. Her fault he might have lost everything he'd worked so hard for.

Stepping up to where she sat, he gathered her chin between his fingers. "Why didn't you tell me the truth? I would have moved Heaven and Earth just to be with you."

"I was afraid." The truth of it was in her voice, the look in her eyes. "I was young. I didn't know any better but to believe every word my father said."

Damn. The truth hit him square in the chest. He had no idea what to say, how to feel. It was too much to digest in one sitting. He'd convinced himself he was better off without Paxton, was sure he knew what kind of woman she was.

But he no longer had any idea of what was right and what wasn't. The one truth he'd carried with him for so long suddenly turned into one huge lie. It filled his head with a million doubts and questions he didn't want to have to deal with at the moment.

"Hunter." The sound of his name held a questioning tone. He lowered his eyes to hers and knew what he wanted.

Memories were dangerous, but her long sleek body was inviting. He could lose himself in her sweetness, forget all about what she'd told him. Making love to her would wipe out the uncertainty for a little while.

Reaching down, he gathered her into his arms, capturing her mouth in a kiss, sweeping them away to a place far removed from reality.

Chapter Sixteen

Paxton wasn't sure what she'd expected after sharing the truth. She'd been prepared for just about anything. Anything, that is, except for the strange distance Hunter put between them as the sun rose, rousing them from a night of making love until their bodies fell into complete exhaustion.

What little sleep they'd accomplished had come in the very early hours of morning. Wrapped tight in his embrace, Hunter had held her to the warmth of his body, making her feel more protected, loved, than she ever had before. She'd woken with a smile on her face, and a burden lifted from her shoulders that had weighed her down for years.

It had been a brief joy, interrupted when he abruptly rolled from his side of bed, claiming they needed a quick start to the day. He'd showered, she'd followed, and during that first passing hour, hardly three full sentences were shared between them. He'd drawn into himself. Though she fought to admit it, she couldn't deny his distance hurt.

"I ordered some breakfast." He turned her way when she came out of the bathroom, damp curls tickling her shoulders.

Nodding, she dumped her wet towel on the bed, and ran her fingers through her hair, pulling out the knots that had formed. He paced the room like a caged tiger searching for escape. His dark eyes were shadowed in thought, and his forehead creased with tension.

"So is this how it's going to be between us?" She couldn't take any more of his silence. She needed answers before she went crazy with not knowing.

He paused in midstride. Sighing, he turned toward her, settled on the edge of the bed. He had yet to put his shirt back on and her eyes flashed to the muscles rippling underneath his bronzed skin.

Gathering her hand into his, he was silent for a moment. Turning her hand palm up, he traced his fingers over the lines etched across the sensitive skin. When he glanced up, confusion clouded his eyes and she instantly laid a comforting hand to his rough cheek.

"I have to be honest with you." He released her hand, turning away to stare at the wall. "I don't know how to react to what you told me."

He sighed, running an agitated hand through his hair. "Part of me wants to jump at a second chance between us and give us another try at what we once had."

Paxton had a sinking feeling in the pit of her stomach. "But—"

He pushed to his feet, again picking up his pace across the room. "But…I don't know if that's possible. The fact is, we're two different people from two different worlds. If we couldn't make it through the first time we were together, how can we make it through a second time?"

"I told you what happened the last time. This time, I wouldn't listen to my father no matter what he threatened. I'm a big girl now. I don't need Daddy making decisions for me anymore."

"It's not that simple." He stopped to stare out the window. "It never was that simple. Your father may have been the reason why we parted, but he wasn't the only problem in our relationship. My background and yours just seem to clash. I don't think we can get past that boundary."

"You're making the boundaries." She moved away from the bed, joining him at the window. His doubtful gaze traveled over her. "Nobody has the perfect relationship, Hunter. Everyone has to get over their differences when they're in love. That's what makes the relationship stronger."

A knock at the door drew his attention away. "I don't know what to do right now," he told her, brushing his knuckles gently across her cheek, before walking to the door. "After I get us out of this mess, we'll talk."

He left her standing alone at the window. She turned to gaze outside, listening with only half an ear to what was being said at the door. She assumed the knock meant the breakfast Hunter ordered had arrived. Yet, she felt no hunger or interest in the meal.

"Ashland thought this might interest you," she heard the young girl at the door tell Hunter before backing out of the room. Several seconds of silence passed before his sudden curse caused her to jump in surprise.

"What's wrong?" She moved to his side.

"Your ex-fiancé is getting desperate." He tossed a newspaper face up onto the table.

Dreading what was next, her eyes strayed to the front page of the paper. She recognized the popular name of the newspaper. It was the major circulation in

Denver and the surrounding areas.

But it wasn't the name of the paper that had her sucking in her breath. Grasping the edge of the table, she steadied suddenly weak knees. Staring back at her through black and white print was a picture of herself, taken a few months ago at a business dinner with Grant and his associates.

In the picture she was tucked in the crook of Grant's arm, talking with another on the opposite side. Though her face appeared at a slight angle, every feature was evident, making it easy for almost anyone to recognize her.

"How did this get here?" She tried hard not to stammer over her words. "We're in Montana, not Colorado."

"It's not unusual for places out here to subscribe to the Denver paper. There are a lot of tourists in this area. Many, like Ashland, bring in the papers from the bigger cities for their guests."

Her gaze fell to her picture, reading the big bold letters making up the headline above. "Grant Robinson seeks the whereabouts of his fiancée. Foul play is suspected in her disappearance on the day of her wedding."

"It's a lie. How could they print something so far from the truth?"

Hunter picked up the paper, his eyes scanning the article following the headlines. "The paper doesn't know it's a lie. I'm sure, with Grant's standing, they were willing to believe whatever he told them."

She reached for the telephone behind her. Her hand closed over the receiver as Hunter wrapped his fingers tightly around her wrist, leaving her no choice but to let go.

"What are you doing?" He pulled her hand away, stepped between her and the telephone.

"I'm calling the editor of the paper, telling them they printed a lie. News must really be slow back in Denver if something like this actually made it as one of the lead stories."

"It made the front page because of this." He moved her further away from the telephone, pointing at the bottom of the article. "Grant's offering a hefty reward for any information to your whereabouts. Money can carry a lot of weight when it comes to making a story."

"I have to call the paper." Worry and anger clashed in her eyes.

"You can't." He guided her to a chair at the table. "All that will do is tip Grant off to where we are. Wait until this all plays out, then the truth will come out."

She stared down without interest at the breakfast he laid out in front of her. She had less of an appetite than she'd possessed before. The mere thought of food made her stomach roll in protest.

Pushing her plate away, she looked at Hunter across the table. "We can't let him get away with this. I'm tired of Grant being the one to call the shots. Tired of having to be the one running when he's the one who's on the wrong side of the law."

"I know it's frustrating, but we don't have much choice. Sooner or later, he'll be brought down. I promise. Until then, we have to bide our time and keep you safe."

She didn't want to bide her time. She was tired of hiding out. Tired of being on the run. It felt as if Grant was winning this terrible game they were trapped in.

She hated being on the losing end. Especially when she was afraid of losing everything when all was over and done with.

****

Neither of them touched their breakfast. While Paxton gathered their plates, placing them in the hall, Hunter called his partner. After the second ring, his voice filled the line.

"I was expecting a call from you," Smith supplied instead of a customary greeting. "I take it you've seen this morning's paper."

"I've seen it. How did that slide through the Bureau's fingers?"

"We didn't know. Grant hasn't formally reported his missing fiancée to the police. If he had, we would have had some control over what the paper printed. As it is, our hands are tied."

Hunter pinched the bridge of his nose, wondered how many other barriers were going to be thrown in his path before this whole thing was over. Grant was a persistent man if not an honorable one.

"I do have some good news for you," Smith continued.

"Let me have it. I'll pay highly for any kind of good news at this point."

"Then you better start making out a large check in my name." There was a hint of humor in his voice, clashing with the tension Hunter battled. "I think you're going to like what I have to tell you."

"What is it?" He watched Paxton as she moved around the room. She really was beautiful. It would be so easy to give her his heart all over again.

"That little tip you collected from Paxton paid off.

We have Tony Billers currently taking an intimate look at the inside of a jail cell. The guy is starting to talk. I don't think he's going to hold out loyalty to his boss much longer."

"You just made my day." He turned his full attention back to the call.

"And I'm not even done yet. Considering the information she gave us was of use, Williams gained approval to get her into a safe house. I have the address written down right here in front of me."

Hunter gathered a pen and paper. As Smith read off the information, he scribbled it down with great relief. Things were slowly turning to their advantage. With Tony in custody and Paxton safely tucked away under the Bureau's care, the degree of danger would ease.

It wouldn't be long until this whole thing came to a close. The end was near, he felt it in his bones.

"Thanks." Promising to call as soon as they reached their destination, he cut off the call and turned to Paxton, who waited with expectation lining her face.

"Well?" She lifted her hands in the air.

"It looks as if the odds are slowly turning in our favor. You were right about Tony Billers. The Bureau has him in custody. It won't be long before he's telling all in order to save his own hide."

"Thank goodness." She sank into the chair she'd occupied earlier. Her shoulders sagged in long needed relief.

"The Bureau also arranged for you to be brought into a safe house until Grant is taken into custody."

"A safe house." Reluctant sapphire eyes raised to meet his. "Like the kind you hear about in movies? Where the bad guys always find you and kill everyone inside?"

Though she kept her voice light, he heard the fear. Settling in the chair next to her, he gathered her hands into his. "I promise, we are much better trained than those in the movies. The one we're headed to is back in Colorado and we've never had any of the bad guys find it."

"Colorado. We're going back." Dread and fear laced her words.

"Where we're headed is far from Denver. It's on the western slope, closer to Grand Junction. I've been there. And I promise, Grant, or anyone working for him, won't be getting through the defenses the Bureau has in place."

"Will there be other agents there?"

Her fear cut through him like a knife. "They're being transported even as we speak. In a couple of days, when we arrive, the place will be completely secured."

Her hands clenched tighter around his. "Are you staying with me? After we get there with the other agents, are you going to have to leave?"

Falling onto his knees in front of her, he reached up, cupping her cheeks in the palm of his hands. "I won't be going anywhere." Using the pad of his thumb, he stroked the rosiness of her cheek. "We're in this together, until the very end."

****

They didn't waste time in starting back for Colorado. Hunter couldn't shake the feeling he had to get Paxton to the safe house as soon as possible. Once there, he knew she'd be safe with the other agents helping him keep the danger away.

The nightmare was coming to an end. He couldn't

be more grateful. If Tony spilled all like he was expected to, it would only be a couple more days before Grant was tucked behind bars where he belonged. Then Paxton could have her life back. And he could have—

His thoughts came to a crashing halt. Where was he going when this was all over? Was he leaving Colorado, going back to the life he'd led before falling into this mess? Or was he staying, to give a second chance with Paxton a try?

He didn't know. He wished the answers would fall into his lap, but as he had learned before, anything involving Paxton never came easily. He had a feeling this decision was going to be one of the hardest he ever had to make.

He loved her. He couldn't deny it. If he was honest, he had to admit he'd never stopped loving her. The emotion had just been tucked away where it couldn't beat down on him day after day.

But was love enough to conquer the differences between them? Differences that had parted them ten years ago. Regardless of what Theodore Walsh had threatened in order to keep Hunter away from his daughter, they still would have never made it, of that he was sure. There were too many obstacles standing in their way. Too many forces pulling them in opposite directions.

They'd been too young to know how to fight against the odds wanting to keep them apart. Older now, were they stronger in their conviction to keep the love they'd found so long ago?

He wished he knew the answer. If he did, his decision would be simple and quick. He'd spend the rest of his life in her arms. Waking up to her every morning and falling asleep with her at his side each night. If he knew for sure they could succeed, he'd waste no time in making Paxton his wife and starting them on a family of their own.

"I'm hungry." Her voice filled the silence of the car. "Suddenly my appetite has returned."

Glancing at the clock on the dashboard, he realized they'd driven straight through the lunch hour. It was already three in the afternoon. At this rate, they'd make it to the cabin by tomorrow evening.

"The next small town we come to, we'll stop and eat."

"Do you think it will be okay?" She turned in her seat, facing him.

"Just because Ashland had a copy of the Denver paper doesn't mean others out here will. We'll find a little old place in the middle of nowhere that would have no interest in what's happening back in Denver."

Reassured, she turned back to the window at her side while Hunter kept his eye out for signs of civilization.

After another half hour, he found what he was looking for. Flipping the blinker, he took the exit ramp, following the signs guiding them into the small town of River City, Wyoming.

As he'd expected, the town was nothing more than a little dot on the road. Main Street housed only half a dozen dusty brick buildings, two of which were boarded up tight. A small diner was sandwiched in between a feed store and a used clothing shop. Easing off the gas, he brought the car to a stop against the curb outside the diner.

"Just to be safe, I think you should put the cap on."

Nodding, she did as he suggested, joining him on the sidewalk, the baseball cap pulled firmly over her hair. Cupping his hand around her elbow, he led her inside. Guiding them to a back booth, he returned the nod of a waitress passing them on the way.

"I'll be right with you folks." She set two plates down in front of the only other customers in the place—an older man and woman, reading their newspapers across from one another.

They both ordered a burger with fries when she returned. Ten minutes later, she set their food down with a promise to check on them in a bit.

Hunter watched Paxton dig into her food, her tongue peeking out to lick away a dot of ketchup caught on her upper lip. Looking at her now—dressed in clothes she'd been forced to wear for more than a day, a face that had gone without a trace of makeup and a mop of honey-blond curls hidden underneath a baseball cap—he saw nothing of the wealthy socialite she was.

The woman sitting in front of him was at complete ease with her surroundings, showing no signs to the fact she didn't normally dine in such a place or that a burger and fries were not her usual fair. She looked as much in her element here as she did back home with her high society friends.

"I can't believe how hungry I was." She released a long, satisfied sigh. Resting back into the worn cushions of the booth, she picked at the few fries left on her plate. "I felt as if I hadn't eaten for a week."

"You certainly had an appetite." He noticed not a single crumb of her hamburger remained. She'd polished it off completely.

"You two ready for your check?" The waitress

cleared away their plates. At his nod, she tore a piece of paper from her pad, placing it in the center of the table before walking away, arms filled with dirty dishes.

"I suppose we should head back out. I'd like to have at least a couple more hours of daylight to drive with."

They paid the bill, and for a moment, it almost felt normal as he reached for Paxton's hand, and they made their way out of the diner like a couple without a worry to hold them down.

Chapter Seventeen

It's almost over.

The thought repeated through Paxton's mind as Hunter guided them down the highway. Night slowly fell, darkening the landscape into eerie shadows.

It's almost over.

The thought was bittersweet, leaving her wondering which emotion was stronger, relief or dread. She'd be more than happy when the whole mess with Grant was over. Nor could she deny the relief that she and Hunter would no longer be on their own as soon as the other agents were brought in to help.

But dread stirred inside as well. What would happen when this was over? She wanted to believe she and Hunter would find a way to give themselves a second chance. That somewhere inside of them was the need to again find the love they'd once shared.

But there was no guarantee on anything. She'd give her very life to have a second chance. Buried deep in her heart was the secret hope that someday they would find their way back together.

Hunter, though, was a different story. What he felt or didn't feel was a mystery. He said he wanted to talk about the two of them once everything was over. Was that good or bad? She didn't know and wasn't sure she wanted to know.

"Another couple of hours then we'll stop for the

night." He pulled into the far left lane, bypassing a slow moving semi.

The dark of the night slowly became complete, leaving only the stars in the clear sky to offer little light along the barren stretch of road. There were no towns or cities where they were. Only long stretches of dusty fields hidden away in the inky blackness.

She looked forward to the time when they finally stopped for the night. This would be their last night alone. Tomorrow, there would be agents hanging around, taking away the privacy she'd come to thrive on in the time they'd been together.

She may have had doubts and questions about what lay ahead for them, but there was one thing she knew she could depend on—the passion that flared between them. Passion she had every intention of rediscovering as soon as they were locked away in some little hotel room for the night.

She might not have a future with him, but she had tonight. She wasn't about to let it go to waste.

"That's not good," Hunter mumbled, more to himself than to her. His words catching her attention, she pulled away from her thoughts.

"What's not good?" Facing him, she stared at his fierce profile illuminated by the glow from the dashboard.

He gazed hard through the rearview mirror. "That car back there is keeping a steady pace with us. It has been for a while."

She turned in her seat and spotted two round headlights poking through the dark. The shape of the other car was nothing more than a shadow.

"Hold on." His foot pressed down on the

accelerator. "I'm going to try speeding up, see if they stay with us."

They picked up speed while she kept a careful watch on the headlights behind them. The car stayed with them, speeding up as well, changing lanes when Hunter did. Whoever it was never let any sort of distance grow, keeping a steady length between the two cars.

"Do you think they're following us?" She turned back, a shiver running up her spine.

He shrugged. "I don't know for sure. But I don't plan on taking any chances. The next turn off we come to, I'll take it and see if they follow us."

She hoped they worried for nothing. She wasn't up for any more excitement, having more than her fair share lately.

A sign for an upcoming exit passed on the right. Hunter eased off the gas as they approached the off ramp. Bending around the edge of the seat to watch the car behind them, she held her breath and waited to see what would happen next.

For a moment, she thought they were safe as the car stayed in its lane instead of following. But at the last minute, just when she was sure they'd overreacted, it swerved in their direction, falling in line behind them as they left the highway.

"Damn." Hunter's fist hit the steering wheel.

Another cold, slick chill ran up her spine. "They are following us."

The nod of his head fell like a rock in her gut. "Make sure your seatbelt is secure," he barked at the same time he gave his own a fierce tug. "I'm going to try and lose them."

Without slowing for the stop sign at the end of the ramp, he yanked the car hard to the right, turning them onto a dark road heading away from the highway. Behind them, the other car did the same, abandoning the distance they'd kept on the highway, closing in on the rear bumper.

She fell back into her seat with the force of the sudden acceleration as Hunter straightened the car from the turn. The sound of tires screeching echoed around them as rubber and pavement rubbed against one another in a frantic rush of speed.

She kept an eye on the headlights behind them, hoping they'd fade away into the distance, praying some miracle would come into play, and get them away safely. But they stuck to their tail end like glue, keeping pace with their car.

"Hold on." He twisted the car down another road. The force of the turn slammed her against the passenger door. She clamped down on the painful yelp rising in response to the jarring through her shoulders.

The car behind them missed the turn, unable to slow down quick enough to follow them. Taking the chance that was granted, he pushed the gas pedal to the floor, tearing through the gravel pebbles into the darkness ahead.

"Maybe we lost them." She hoped when she saw no sight of the headlights.

"I doubt it." He shook his head, keeping up a steady pace down the dark, deserted road. "It won't be long before they turn around and find their way back."

As if in response to his words, two round lights broke through the darkness. But this time they weren't coming at them from the back end.

"Damn," he growled as the two beams peered at them from the side of the car. "They cut through the field. They're headed right toward us."

They grew closer by the second. It didn't matter how hard Hunter pushed the car, it still wasn't able to outrun the other vehicle headed for them. She braced herself, knowing it was only a matter of time until they caught up. Terror ripped through her as she imagined what would happen when they finally reached them.

The first jolt of metal hitting metal sent the steering wheel spinning out of Hunter's control. Paxton clamped her hands desperately around the handle of the door as the car began to spin. Struggling, he jerked the steering wheel back into his possession, straightening the tires out seconds before they dipped dangerously into the ditch on the side of the road.

Her sigh of relief was short-lived as again the front fender of the other car mated with the back end of their own. The awful sound of crunching metal echoed as they were shoved off the road and into the field.

There was no control as they skid down an embankment, tossing them around like a couple of ragdolls. Out of the night shadows, the dark outline of a tree appeared.

Hunter's hands grasped wildly for the steering wheel, doing everything in his power to keep them from hitting the tree. Paxton's knuckles turned white around the edge of her seat as the car skid along the soft ground, bringing the fateful tree closer.

"Got it." The muscles in his arms bunched with strength as he fought to keep his grip on the steering wheel.

But he was too late. There wasn't enough time to

turn away. Her breath caught painfully behind her ribs as they barreled forward. She heard the sound of impact, front fender buckling underneath the powerful mass of the trunk.

Even with her seatbelt tightened around her middle, she jerked forward. The shoulder belt yanked her painfully back against the seat, tossing her head carelessly against the headrest. Crying out, she felt tears of pain sliding down her cheek. Her legs bumped hard against metal as the wind was knocked painfully from her lungs.

Silence, thick and frightening, settled as the car finally came to a stop. For a second, she couldn't move, couldn't speak. Her chest hurt where the seatbelt cut into her skin. Her neck ached from the lash of force that had tossed it back against the headrest.

Her hands shook and even cupping them together in her lap didn't help stop it. Blood pulsed frantically through her veins, every breath quick and urgent.

"Paxton," Hunter's voice washed over her. "Are you okay?"

"I don't know. I'm afraid to move and find out."

"We have to get out of the car. They'll be coming after us. We're sitting ducks inside here."

She nodded, though she couldn't imagine moving a muscle. He reached over to release her seatbelt before undoing his own. After crawling out of the car, he bolted to her side, and held his hand out in encouragement to get her moving.

She bit down on her bottom lip and tasted the blood that trickled from where her teeth dug into tender flesh, but she didn't care. The pain distracted her from the rest of the torture shooting through her body.

He pulled her from her seat. Her knee screamed in protest as she attempted to straighten her legs, bringing an even tighter hold on her bottom lip, fighting off the tears threatening to escape. Once both feet were flat on the ground, he pulled her to him, holding her up while his arms folded protectively around her.

"Stay close to me," he whispered in her ear, lacing his fingers with hers. At her nod, he tugged on her arm, turning them away from the mangled car, into the darkness looming ahead.

They only made it a few steps before an ugly sneering voice broke through the quiet. "Going somewhere?" The voice rumbled over them, stopping Hunter in his trucks.

She dared a look, a gasp falling from her lips when she caught the glint of a gun pushed tight against Hunter's left temple. Another figure emerged from the shadows, slipping up to her side.

She cringed in disgust as his hand curled around her arm. "Looks like we got them this time." The man at her side yanked hard, attacking muscles already sore from the crash, snatching her from Hunter's hold. He pulled both arms behind her back, pinning them together at her wrists with one large hand.

"Nowhere for you to run is there." The other one shoved his gun deeper into Hunter's forehead. His finger tightened against the trigger and Paxton's breathing stopped.

He wouldn't kill him…would he?

For several seconds, her heart froze as she watched, waited, fear pounding through her veins. If they shot Hunter they might as well go ahead and shoot her too. She had every intention of going after whoever pulled the trigger, even if it meant her own life was lost.

"Boss will be happy with us," the man holding Paxton sneered viciously. "We did what nobody else could. We got his two prize enemies. And it wasn't even that hard."

"I should just do away with this one." The other one patted Hunter down, found his gun, and tossed it deep into the trees. "He ain't no good to anyone."

"Boss wants them both alive. You shoot him, he's gonna come after both of us."

"Makes no sense to me but I'm guessing you're right." He didn't look happy about it.

She breathed a sigh of relief as his finger slipped away from the trigger only to have it turn into a cry of terror as he lifted the butt of his gun and brought it down to the back of Hunter's head. With one swift jolt, he was knocked unconscious, tumbling like a rag to the ground at the man's feet.

"You bastard." She wrestled with her captor in a vain attempt to get away. "How could you do such a thing?"

With a slimy smile, he stepped up to where she arched her body away from his partner. Between his thumbs, he captured her chin, holding her steady with his dark, menacing gaze. "I can do what I please, pretty one. Boss's only instructions were to bring you to him alive. He's still alive, ain't he?"

He hovered close, the stench of his warm breath washing over her, forcing her to swallow down a wave of nausea. "Maybe I'll have some fun with you too. The boss never said nothing about keeping my hands to myself. And you look like you'd be awfully fun to be touching. Maybe I could even learn what it was that got the boss so interested in you."

She wanted to curse at him. Wanted to spit in his face, tell him just what she thought of him. But an inner instinct warned her against such an emotional display. She had a feeling a man like him played on a woman's emotions. Any show of anger and resentment he earned from her would only push him to go further with his threats.

And threats were all they were. She didn't believe either one of them would risk Grant's wrath by trying something with her. Neither of them knew exactly the depths of their boss's feelings for his fiancée and they didn't want to risk finding out. Of that, she was sure.

"Let's get them back to the car." He spun away after another minute without any response from her. Obviously, the game was no fun when she didn't want to play.

Curling his hands underneath Hunter's shoulders, the goon dragged his limp body up the embankment while Paxton was pushed along behind him. She cringed each time he was yanked over a rock without so much as a pause in movement. His limp form bounced carelessly over the rough ground, twigs and dried weeds reaching out, scratching his bare skin.

Hunter's unconscious body was shoved into the back seat, and Paxton was pushed roughly over him. As soon as the door slammed shut behind her, she scampered into a sitting position, collecting his head into her lap.

She caressed his cheeks, leaving tiny kisses along his cool skin. He stirred for a moment as the car kicked to life but then fell silent again as they turned back onto the road, shooting off into the night to an unknown destination.

****

A freight train barreled through Hunter's head. He ground his teeth together, trying to fight off the pain rumbling inside. He wasn't sure where he was or what was going on. The only thing he was certain of was that he was going to have one heck of a headache for the next few hours.

Slowly, his eyes slid open. Above him, the gentle shape of Paxton's face came into focus. Her forehead creased in worry, and silent tears slipped from her sapphire eyes. He tried reaching up to rub away the lines of worry but found he couldn't move a muscle.

"Paxton." It was a chore just to get her name through his lips. It came out as no more than a whisper, but it was enough. Her eyes came to his, a small smile forming on her lips as she looked down on him.

"You're awake." She brushed his hair from his eyes and bent over, leaving a soft kiss on his brow. "How are you feeling?"

"Terrible," he said through clenched teeth, the effort leaving him breathless.

"Where…where are we?" He was aware of the feeling of motion beneath him.

"I don't know." She turned away. "We've been driving through the night and still they aren't slowing down."

Driving. They were in a car. Slowly, realization settled through his bones. He remembered the tree, the gun held to his head. Remembered the fright in Paxton's eyes seconds before the world went blank. The bastards had knocked him out cold, leaving her to fend with the slime on her own.

"Are you okay?" He stroked her arm. The thought of what they might have done to her while he lay unconscious sent murder racing through his blood.

She nodded. "I'm fine. They treated me a whole lot better than they did you."

"Are you sure? They didn't hurt you?" He wasn't convinced. The fear of her alone and vulnerable was almost too much to handle.

"No." She shook her head. "They didn't hurt me."

Relief washed over him, dousing the angry flames that had burned only seconds before. With an agonized groan, he rolled from her lap, getting a look out the window behind them. The sun was slowly beginning to grace the eastern sky, chasing away the darkness of night. They were traveling along a long stretch of highway that looked as barren and isolated as the one they'd been on the day before.

"Well, look who's awake."

Hunter's head shot around at the sound of the unfamiliar voice. A man, as dark and dangerous as they came, peered around the edge of the passenger seat. Instantly, Paxton's arms tightened around him.

"Where are you taking us," he demanded, his hand coming up to take hers.

"I don't see how that's any of your business. Just sit back and relax. We'll be there soon enough."

He bit down on the angry retort coming to mind. Agitating these two would do no good. He'd have to bide his time until they reached their destination. He wasn't sure what to expect or what was going to happen once they arrived. All he knew was he was going to do everything within his power to get him and Paxton out of this alive.

Especially Paxton. He'd give his life if it meant saving hers.

Sitting back against the seat, he gathered her into the crook of his arm, cuddling her to his side. She rested her head against his chest, angling her body to connect tightly with his. She shuddered and he knew she was frightened but was doing her best to try to hold it back. His strong Paxton. She was going to stand tall to the very end, regardless of what they did to them.

"We're going to get through this," he whispered in her ear so his words wouldn't be overheard. "We've gotten this far. I don't plan on giving up yet."

Sapphire eyes, clear and trusting, met his without reluctance. Smiling, she flattened her soft palm against his rough cheek. "I know we will…together."

Chapter Eighteen

"Road trip is over."

The man in the passenger seat interrupted the silent moments they'd shared through the long journey across the Wyoming landscape into the rocky terrain of the Colorado Mountains. They had traveled through the day but weren't aware of the time that had lapsed.

Their attention was focused on each other, leaving no room for other thoughts. They hadn't talked. Had only held tight to each other, gathering the strength they needed to face what lay ahead.

"Looks like your host is waiting for you." He climbed from the front of the car. His hand rested on the handle of the back door waiting for the driver to climb out and grab the opposite side.

Seconds later, Paxton and Hunter were separated. Grabbed roughly out of opposite sides of the car and pushed toward a dark image lingering on the front porch of a sprawling mountain home, which blended into the wilderness around it.

The driver took hold of Hunter, a grip meant to keep him from trying anything funny. The other man grabbed painfully onto Paxton's elbow, steering her along. Their footsteps ground against the pebble drive, the sound echoing through the quiet of the mountains. From across the top of the car, she caught Hunter's look of warning. For the time being, they had to go along with whatever happened.

On the front porch, Grant waited. She took a good look at him, as she was shoved along, bile rising in her throat at the sight of the man she'd almost married. Hatred unlike any she'd known burned inside. Hatred for not only the secrets he'd kept from her, the deception she'd almost married into, but also the danger he tossed her and Hunter into the middle of.

Dark eyes, almost a pure black, traced their progress across the front drive, and then rested on Paxton with an evil sneer. Gone was any trace of the man she'd once known, replaced by what she was sure was the true Grant Robinson.

He was dark, foreboding. Hard lines creased his shadowed face, and evil danced in his eyes. An evil so strong, she shuddered from its force.

How had she not noticed it before? Grant must have perfected the other man he portrayed while courting her. The man who had always been somewhat cool and distant but had never appeared as dark and dangerous as he did at that moment.

"I've missed you, my dear," he sneered when they were face to face. His cold hand wrapped around her arm and jerked her to his side. She cringed as he placed a heavy arm around her shoulders to pull her closer.

"You used to like my touch." Cold, expressionless eyes looked down on her. With the pad of his thumb, he stroked a line down the curve of her cheek. It took all of her resolve not to punch him in the gut and show him just how much she liked his touch.

Being close to him sickened her. He was a stranger as far as she was concerned. A stranger she had every reason to fear.

"And this must be lover boy," he continued, as Hunter was shoved toward him. "Your daddy told me about the bit of rebellion you shared with him. He isn't happy you two are together. That's why he was kind enough to help me locate you. He knew I was the only man for you."

Unable to stand him a second longer, she flattened her palms against his chest, and shoved, breaking free from the arm around her shoulders. "If my father knew the truth about you, he would have never helped you find me."

To her relief, he didn't reach out for her again. She glued herself to Hunter's side. He swept his arm around her shoulders, and she sank into his familiar hold, thankful for the strength she was able to draw from his presence.

"There are very few people who know the truth about me, Paxton, dear. And I intend to keep it that way. I haven't come this far to let a little pest like you ruin me."

"You're already ruined. No matter what you do to us, it won't change the fact you're about to be found out."

"Ah, yes." Grant rubbed the bottom of his chin as if in great thought. "You're thinking of Tony, aren't you? I figured you had a hand in his arrest since not many people know of his existence."

"They do now."

An unconcerned shrug lifted his shoulders. "He can do me no harm. I already have plans to take care of him just as I did the last informant who tried to take me down."

"But Tony was your friend," Paxton protested in

disbelief. "You intend to kill someone you've been close to for so many years."

Reaching out, Grant trailed a finger along the shape of her lips, flashing a knowing smile when she stepped away from him, and deepened her embrace with Hunter. "Haven't you figured it out? I don't allow myself to care for anyone, not even Tony. Such emotions only get in the way. They're sloppy, and I don't have time for sloppiness."

"You're a sick man, Grant. I can't believe I didn't see the truth about you earlier."

"Not sick, my dear, just smart." His answering smile was enough to raise goose bumps on her arms.

There were a million arguments she could give, but the effort would be useless. Grant's mind had its own way of thinking, closing out any kind of sane reason trying to break through. For once, she fully understood the meaning of a madman.

She shivered with the thought of what he was capable of. The man had no conscience. No grasp on the concept of right or wrong. She'd known he was the one responsible for her life being in danger. But it wasn't until coming face to face with him she finally realized how cold and ruthless he truly was.

The men with the guns who had come after her and Hunter time and again were not the ones who wanted her dead. They were nothing more than runners for Grant, who set out to kill the woman he claimed he loved. He wanted her dead. She meant no more to him than Tony who would surely find the same fate as well.

"Shall I have my assistants escort you in?" He waved at the two men as they stepped out of the shadows. "Or can I trust you two will find your own way without any stupid tricks."

The squeeze around Paxton's shoulders prodded her into answering for the both of them. "We don't need help from your assistants," she drawled with sarcasm. "They've already proven to be enough help, thank you."

"Very well." He turned his back, slowly pushing on the heavy wooden door. It didn't make a sound as it rolled on the hinges, swinging open, allowing them entry into the large house.

Though Paxton had brushed away the help of his assistants, they fell into step behind her and Hunter, staying close on their heels until they were safely closed away inside the house. The heavy door closed with a low thud. Her heart sank as one of the men locked it tight, tucking the keys into his pocket.

The interior of the house was dark with shadows. Though there were many windows, not a single curtain was left open to allow sunlight to settle in. A chill hovered in the air. A deathly silence reverberated through the rooms.

"Dinner will be served promptly at seven," Grant informed them, hitching one foot on the bottom of a large staircase. "I can assure you that your final meal will be elegant and grand. I always treat my guests with the utmost respect."

"You mean your prisoners," Paxton bit off before she was able to stop herself. She knew angering him would do no good. But she couldn't force herself to participate in whatever sick game he was playing.

He stepped forward, stopping only inches away from where she stood. Squaring her shoulders, she fought the urge to back away, knowing it would only give him more satisfaction.

"I don't keep prisoners." With a cold hand, he trailed a line down the length of her arm, circling her wrist before retracing his path back up to her shoulder. "Even my worst enemies are considered my guests as long as they are inside my home."

Black eyes met hers, holding her in a deep, evil spell she couldn't break free from. In that moment, she saw the hatred burning inside his soul. A hatred for anyone who dared betray him. Running so deep it controlled every thought in his mind.

"My assistants will show you to your room." He broke the spell and stepped away. "I expect you will be presentable by the time they come back for you."

He turned away, disappearing down a long hallway. One of the two men stepped up in his place, holding out his arm in invitation for them to climb the stairs. At the top, they were guided down a long, winding hallway to a room at the far end. The door was swept open, and they were led into a large suite of rooms, rich and elegant enough for royalty.

"You should find clothes inside the closet and all your other necessities in the bathroom." They backed out the door, locking it firmly behind them.

Because she couldn't resist, Paxton reached out, gave the knob a twist, but knew it was a waste of time. Opening the curtains, she found not only were they looking at a hefty drop toward the ground below, but also thick bars attached to the windows prevented any hope of escape.

They were trapped, closed away inside the room until called upon to face their deaths.

****

Hunter watched Paxton sink into the cushions of a lavish leather couch occupying the entire right corner of the room. He read the despair etched deep across her face. Regardless of what they'd promised during the long drive, it was hard to keep up hope when faced with what looked like an impossible situation.

He'd kept his silence around Grant, uttering not a word. He knew anything he had to say would only help increase the anger seething inside Paxton's ex-fiancé. It was well-learned instinct keeping him quiet when Grant touched Paxton, and helping him shove down his burning need to tell the bastard what he thought of him.

But his silence didn't mean he'd given in. Grant may have plans for them, but he was going to do everything within his power to alter those plans to their advantage. He hadn't gotten them this far to lose everything now. Every stubborn bone inside toughened even more, straightened his spine into a rod of steel, and squared his shoulders into a tough line of determination.

It was time somebody knocked Grant Robinson off his self-imposed pedestal. The man would go down, he'd make sure of it. And he'd take great pleasure in watching him fall.

Paxton collapsed into his hold when he joined her on the couch, resting a weary head on his shoulder. "There's no way for us to get out of here." Hunter strained to hear her quiet words. "We're trapped."

"We're together." He pulled her closer. "That alone gives us an advantage Grant doesn't have."

"How? He's the one with those dangerously armed goons backing him up. What do we have?"

With the tip of his finger, he tilted her small chin,

lifting her gaze to his. "We have patience. Grant is cocky. Too sure of himself. He's bound to trip up. When he does, I'll be ready. All we have to do is wait for him to make that one fatal mistake."

"And if he doesn't?"

"He will. I'm sure of it." He hoped she believed him.

She rested her head against his shoulders. He lifted his hand to the long flow of her honey-blond hair, running his fingers through the silky strands. Her soft scent enveloped him as her supple body pressed against his.

He tightened in response but bit down hard on the desire washing through his bones. She didn't need that from him, not now. What she needed was his strength and assurance to lean on. She needed him to offer comfort against the evils haunting her and the unknown looming ahead.

Later, he'd act on his other feelings while he discovered her sweet body all over again. And when he did, he planned to take his sweet time, making up for all they were missing due to the uncertainty clouding them.

"Paxton." He lifted her gaze to his. Sapphire eyes, damp with unshed tears, met his, tearing a hole through his heart. He hated to see her frightened. Hated to think of anyone placing such fear inside her. His resolve to watch Grant fall, and fall hard, multiplied in intensity.

"I need you to make me a promise." He tightened his arm around her shoulders.

She nodded, weak and unsure.

"No matter what happens, I need you to trust me enough to do whatever I ask. No matter what it is. I don't know what to expect when they come calling for us. But I need to know I can count on you to go along with whatever has to happen."

Pushing up, she placed a gentle kiss on his rough cheek. "I trust you," she spoke with a firm tone and an earnest shimmer in her eyes. "You have my promise to do whatever you need. If anyone can get us out of this, you can. I won't doubt a word you say."

"Good." He placed a firm kiss on her lips. "Because I will get us out of this. I promise. In my job, the good guys always win."

"Always?" Innocent eyes looked back at him.

"As far as I'm concerned, they do. Even when it doesn't look that way, in the end, the bad guys always turn up the losers."

"Good, because I want to see Grant pay for everything he's done. To us…to everyone else who has been unfortunate enough to cross his path."

"Me too, princess. Me too."

Chapter Nineteen

Keeping with his strict control to have everything around him run perfectly, Grant had carefully planned their dinner. The clothes he'd provided were nowhere close to what they'd been wearing. Instead, there was a navy blue, three-piece suit for Hunter. A cocktail dress in red sequin for Paxton.

"Obviously, we're expected to dress for dinner." Hunter hooked the hangers over his fingers and backed out of the closet. He handed Paxton her dress and slung his suit over his arm.

The hours locked inside the room passed by much too quickly. Through the open curtains, Paxton watched the sun slowly lower in the western sky until it peeked over the mountaintops, preparing for its final plunge into darkness. They'd waited until the last possible minute before looking to see what Grant left inside the closet for them. And with the gown slung over her arm, she wished they'd waited even longer.

After such a long stretch of time living in cotton shirts and shorts, she had no desire to put on a gown that would itch at her all night long. It was stiff and uncomfortable just to look at. She knew from experience it would be no better when she finally had it on.

"He definitely thought of everything." Hunter tossed a pair of nylons and red heels on the floor next to her feet.

"Shoes for me too." He held up a pair of black oxfords.

"I don't see why we should even bother with dressing up," she spat in a last bit of rebellion, flinging the dress carelessly along the couch. "All we're doing is playing along with Grant's sick game. Shouldn't we be playing against him instead of with him?"

Hunter lifted the dress with one finger, holding it out to her until she reluctantly accepted it. "Right now, our best bet is to keep him thinking he has the upper hand."

"He does have the upper hand, Hunter." She shot a disgusted look his way while she fought back the frightened tears.

"Only temporarily." Without an ounce of modesty, he stripped away his clothes, baring bronzed skin to her suddenly eager eyes. "He will trip up. I can guarantee you that. The man is too damn confident in himself not to make some sort of mistake."

She wanted to answer but found she couldn't utter a word. Danger might be staring them straight in the face, the fate of their lives might be hanging in the balance of unknown, but none of that mattered at the moment. The only thing she found she could concentrate on was the affect Hunter's naked body was having over her.

Even now, even after they had rediscovered one another all over again, the sight of him still had the ability to render her speechless, to make her aware, in so many places, what he was capable of doing to her. Her hands itched to reach out and touch his dark, muscled skin. Her lips burned to taste him. It was all she could do not to act on the impulses racing through her body. It took every ounce of self-control to turn away and concentrate on getting her own clothes on.

She stripped down naked and was in the process of sliding the silky nylons up her legs, when long, strong arms wrapped around her from behind.

Hunter's hands clasped around her waist and pulled her back against his broad chest. "If you only knew how badly I want to make love to right now," he whispered hoarsely in her ear, his breath kicking up a lock of hair and tickling her neck. "I want nothing more than to toss you down on that bed we saw in the other room and ravish your body until we are both pleading for mercy."

His words brought a burning to her core, making her want with the fury she'd turned away from only minutes before. She twisted in his arms, bare breasts pressing against the stiff material of his jacket. Disappointment hit as she realized he'd finished dressing.

Had he still been bared to her touch, she knew there would be no avoiding the temptation. She would have easily forgotten about the minutes ticking by and taken the delight he promised.

"You should know better than to undress in front of me, princess." He nipped at the small lobe of her ear. "That's one temptation I can't resist."

She wound her arms around his neck, placing a quick kiss on the tip of his nose. "Look who's talking. You almost killed me when you started stripping your clothes away. It was all I could do not to attack you right then and there."

"Soon." He swept his lips across hers. "Very soon,

I'm going to show you just what you do to me. The minute we get out of this mess, we're going to lock ourselves away for a good week. Do nothing but make love all day and all night, until we can't take another second."

"I'm going to hold you to that." She pushed back the request for another promise. One involving the two of them and their future together.

Reluctantly, she stepped out of his hold. His dark eyes continued to follow her as she slipped the dress over her shoulders and straightened the long lines over her hips. Seconds later, they were both ready and waiting for the inevitable.

Footsteps echoed through the hall twenty minutes later, sending a chill up Paxton's spine. She burrowed even deeper against Hunter's side for protection. She knew she couldn't be a coward. Her life, and Hunter's life, depended on her courage, her strength, for the next few hours. But until that door opened and they were escorted away, she was going to take advantage of the one chance to let her true fears show.

"Paxton." Hunter's hands closed around both sides of her face. "Remember what I said. We can get through this. Trust me on that."

"I do trust you. I trust you with my heart and soul."

His mouth found hers in one final desperate kiss. She clung to him desperately, never wanting to let go as their lips ignited with the unspoken words between them. In that kiss, they shared their fears, their courage. Their weaknesses and their strengths. As their lips met, so did their souls, binding them together for the fight they were about to face.

The sound of the creaking doorknob pulled them

apart.

"I love you," he gave on a ragged breath as the door swung open and their privacy ended.

Stepping into the doorway, the same two men from before passed dark looks over them. Paxton was getting tired of seeing them. But then, they were a better sight than Grant was sure to be.

"Good, you're ready." The shorter of the two nodded. "The boss hates his guests being late for dinner. He's a stickler for everything running perfectly on time."

Approaching Hunter, he turned to the other man hovering in the doorway. "You take the little fiancée." He wrapped a hand around Hunter's arm. "These two have had some time to think out their escape plans. I don't trust either of them to not try something funny on the way down to the dining room."

His slick gaze passed over Paxton, making her cringe. Stepping up, he took her arm, and waited until the other man led Hunter out before falling into step behind them. He paused only long enough to close the door before pushing her down the hallway toward the stairs that would take them to Grant.

****

"I trust you with my heart and soul."

Paxton's words repeated inside Hunter's head as they stepped into a candlelit dining room with classical music flowing in the background. At one end of a long mahogany table sat Grant

Dressed in his own three-piece suit, sipping from a glass of dark-red wine, he rose as they were brought into the room. Waving his hands at his sides, he directed them to their places.

Once seated on either side of him, he dismissed the other two with a flick of his wrist. "There is other business to tend to," he told them in a final order before they disappeared. "I expect to hear from you by tomorrow morning with a complete account of what you have taken care of."

They nodded before slipping out the door. Their footsteps echoed back into the dining room as they descended the hall.

"They're leaving?" Paxton's voice was filled with surprise.

"They are of no use to me here. There is business back in Denver that needs tended to."

"You mean Tony," Paxton guessed, receiving a nod in answer.

"But that is not of our concern this evening." He poured two glasses of wine from the bottle at his side then handed them each one. "The cook has left us a tremendous meal before leaving for the weekend. I would hate to disappoint her by letting any of it go to waste."

Hunter absorbed each tiny bit of information Grant was feeding them. From what he could surmise, they were alone in the house. The cook had left. The other two were on their way to Denver. Unless there were more he knew nothing about, Grant had made his first fatal mistake.

The odds evened up, there was more of a chance sitting in his and Paxton's corner. With his confidence in himself, Grant had opened a wide vulnerable hole for him to work with.

"I do hope you enjoy your dinner," Grant continued, passing the dishes huddled in the center of the table. "I made sure you were given an extra special offering this evening, considering it will be your last meal."

"Do you have to go through with this Grant?" Paxton shook her head at the dish of buttered peas he offered. "If you actually plan on killing us, why waste time with this little game of yours? Wouldn't it just be easier to get it over with?"

Hunter understood where her question was coming from. Impatience was wearing on him as well. But he knew enough about Grant's kind to know they had no choice but to wait him out. Men like him enjoyed toying with their intended victims. It was their way to flex their muscles. Show they were the ones in control and calling all the shots.

Grant was enjoying every minute of this. In his own sick mind, he saw it as a form of torture. A way to let the worry of death eat away at his dinner guests until they were almost overwhelmed by it. And only then did he plan to pull his final card out of the hat.

They were definitely not the first ones Grant had treated to such an evening. How many more had sat at this table with the promise of death hanging over their heads? Hunter began to wonder how many counts of murder they could actually bring against the man. Probably more than the Bureau ever suspected.

"You have yourself quite an operation going." Hunter spoke for the first time. The sound of his voice pulled Grant's surprised attention in his direction.

"Well...the lover boy does speak. I was beginning to wonder if you had a voice, or if your attributes were limited only to the bedroom."

"I can assure you I can be very vocal if I choose to

be."

"I'm sure you can," Grant returned with a nod. "I've done some checking into you, Hunter Reese. You're not just Paxton's ex-lover. Your interest in me is much more diverse than that. You're one of those annoying agents who thinks he can put me behind bars. Believes they can actually get the upper hand with me."

A laugh, void of humor, filled the room. "I guess tonight is the night I get my cake and eat it too. You'll be a double treat to get rid of, Mr. Reese."

Hunter watched anger bubble inside Paxton. Before he was able to direct a warning look across the table, her fork slammed hard on her plate, blazing eyes meeting Grant in a rise of fury.

"You have no right to threaten him." Her voice rose a notch with each word. "He's a better man than you will ever be."

Still as calm as ever, Grant flashed her an unconcerned grin. "I could argue with you on that one, but my food is getting cold. I do not desire to let such a meal go to waste because of an argument with you."

She opened her mouth to speak again, but this time Hunter was able to stop her with a small shake of his head before she let another tirade of words escape. Grant turned back to his meal, paying no attention to the other two at the table.

Hunter hardly noticed the food before him. His attention stayed on Paxton across the table. Every protective instinct inside was running on overdrive. If Grant so much as harmed a single hair on her pretty head, he wasn't exactly sure he could stop himself from killing the man. He'd already brought enough terror down on her shoulders. There wasn't much more he was willing to let Grant get away with.

He loved Paxton.

It was that simple of an explanation. He may have no answers yet for the future that may or may not lay ahead of them. He had no idea what risks he was willing to take where she was concerned. But he could no longer deny the fact his feelings ran as deep, if not deeper, than they had the first time he'd fallen in love with her.

If he could only risk his heart one more time, believe in the love they'd found again. Maybe then they'd actually have the future he'd dreamed for them so long ago. Maybe then they could learn the meaning of forever.

Stuffing such thoughts back in the corner of his mind where they belonged, he forced his concentration on the matter at hand. Nothing mattered if he didn't get them out of the current mess they were in. His first concern had to be how to get them out of Grant's clutches with their lives still intact. Later, there would be time to ponder other things.

"It looks as if you don't have much of an appetite tonight, my dear." Grant shook his head at Paxton, her plate still full on the table. "I made sure the cook created some of your favorite dishes. I'm rather disappointed you didn't enjoy them."

"Enough." Her open palm slapped against the hard wood of the table. "You know damn well why I have no appetite. I refuse to put up with another second of your insane comments."

The hand flying across the table, grabbing Paxton's wrist, was swift enough to be nothing but a pale blur to Hunter's eyes. The second she cringed in pain from the pressure squeezing around her tender skin, he was on his feet.

"You are in no position to be arguing with me, my dear." Grant tugged on her arm, holding up a warning hand to Hunter's quick approach. "Your boyfriend and you are under my control. Do you understand that? I set the rules, not you."

His carefully controlled temper was slipping. Hunter saw it in the flash of anger in his eyes and the tightening of his usually lax shoulders. His guests weren't reacting in the way he wanted. They weren't cowering from the fear of death he promised. Refused to beg for their life, as he was sure many had done in the past.

No. They would not give him the fear he thrived on and that was a twist in the plans he hadn't counted on.

Mistake number two for Grant Robinson.

****

Paxton's wrist burned with pain. Grant's fingers were unforgiving as they twisted around her slender bones. A rage she had never seen before lit his black eyes, and there was a twitch to his bottom lip that truly did not become the man.

"I'm done being pleasant with the two of you." He yanked again on her arm. She bit down on her bottom lip, fighting the painful cry threatening to escape. She wasn't going to give him the satisfaction of letting him know he was hurting her.

Hunter shoved his large body between her and Grant, forcing him to let go of her. The second her wrist was free, she cradled it with her other hand, knowing the red welts that were forming would turn into ugly bruises before long.

Without turning his back on Grant, he reached behind him, finding, and clasping Paxton's hands into his own. "I think we're all a little tired of this. Why don't you call in your goons and get this over with?"

"I'll be taking care of my own business tonight. It's just the three of us left to settle the score."

Hunter's shoulders squared in satisfaction. Paxton wondered what she'd missed. Something Grant said held some interest to him. But the only thing she could think about was that the horror had just begun. She was already struggling to hold on to what was left of her quickly fading courage.

"I think it's time for us to take a little walk."

Though she expected Grant to be armed, her eyes still widened in surprise when his hand disappeared behind his back, returning with a long, threatening gun. He waved it at them, motioning toward the other side of the room where a single door separated them from the outside world.

"I always enjoy an evening stroll during the summer months," he talked carelessly as they moved together across the room. "Especially out here in the wide open wilderness where it's only you and the trees."

"How many of your other guests have taken this walk?" Hunter kept a steady grip on her hand as they stepped out into the thick blackness of the night.

"Enough to know your bodies will never be found." His smile was pure evil. Hatred shimmered hot in his dark eyes.

She cringed at the image he presented. They weren't the first ones he'd taken out here to die. And if he succeeded in doing away with them, they more than likely wouldn't be the last.

How could this man have fooled her so completely? How could she not have seen him for the cold-hearted killer he was? She couldn't believe she had been that blind to the truth, too naïve to realize the true man behind the façade he presented to the rest of the world.

Her only defense was she hadn't tried very hard to get to know him. Not in the way she should have considering she had agreed to marry him. It wasn't a big shock to realize Grant was the perfect fiancé for Theodore Walsh's preference, not his daughter's. On the outside, he had made a perfect picture. That was all that her father needed to see to convince him he was the man for Paxton.

Ten years ago, in Hunter, he'd seen a young man trying to seduce his daughter. A man who held none of the qualities Theodore Walsh was convinced his daughter must have in a husband. He came from the wrong background. The wrong kind of family. There was no money to his name or prestige associated with his family. He was a nobody. A boy who had grown up on the seedier side of the streets. As far as her father was concerned, that was reason enough to keep the two of them apart.

And she'd let him do just that. Allowed him to map out her life, take away the one person who had found a special place in her heart. How ironic it was that the man her father so strongly decided was wrong for his daughter was the very man putting his life on the line to protect her from Theodore Walsh's opinion of the perfect husband.

"Hope you two have your energy stored up," Grant

carried on as if they were nothing more than a few friends out for a casual stroll. "We have a lengthy walk ahead of us."

He poked the gun in their direction, keeping them moving forward toward a small path carved between long, thick branches of towering trees. "I don't advise trying anything funny. I have a very itchy trigger finger and plan to be right on your heels, the gun pointed directly at your backs. Any strange moves, you'll both go down before you know what's happening."

Hunter slipped his fingers through Paxton's, tugging her close to his side as they moved through the dark shadows of the trees. Once they'd moved out of range of the house and its guiding lights, Grant withdrew a flashlight from his belt, and aimed the beam in front of them, lighting their way on the rocky terrain.

"Stay as close to me as you can," he whispered, avoiding Grant's range of hearing.

She nodded, stepping even closer to the warmth of his body. Whatever happened tonight, she knew she would never regret the second chance they'd been given. To find Hunter again, love him again, made her life complete.

****

Grant hadn't lied when he promised a long walk. It was a hard hike up the side of a mountain, crisscrossing between hundred-year-old trees, and large boulders pushing from the hard earth. Only the flashlight and the few stars visible through the long branches offered light to guide their way. Paxton held tight to Hunter's hand, using the stability of his hold to help keep her balance over the obstacles lying at their feet.

Her legs began to ache from the exertion of

climbing straight uphill in a pair of high-heeled shoes. Her lungs burned with the chill of the night air sucked in with each labored breath. Wherever Grant was taking them, he was taking extra care to make sure they were buried deep away from civilization.

When she felt as if she couldn't take another second, they broke out into a small clearing, mountain growth no longer grabbing at them from all sides.

"That's far enough," Grant commanded from behind, dropping the beam of the flashlight. The path in front of them suddenly plunged into darkness.

From behind, she heard the shuffling of footsteps as his heavy shoes crunched on the pebbles and dry leaves littering the ground. He circled around, never letting the gun waver from its threatening aim.

An ugly sneer crawled up his face as he stood in front of them. "I guess the time has come for us to say goodbye. Don't worry, though, I promise not to shed too many tears over your deaths."

Her heart pounded painfully against her chest, keeping time with the terror welling inside. She tried swallowing her fear and reminding herself Hunter promised they'd get out of this alive. But it was proving difficult to do so as she stood in the darkness with a madman holding a gun on her.

Hunter tugged on her hand, bringing her gaze up to meet his. "Trust me," he mouthed before placing a kiss on her lips. She clung to him, desperate to feel his warmth invade the cold fear taking over. His lips melted with hers, taking, and giving every bit of the love they'd never truly lost in all the years they'd been apart.

"My heart is breaking, I assure you." The ugly

sound of Grant's voice intruded. Cold fingers wrapped around Paxton's arm. Yanked away from Hunter's protective hold, she tumbled into Grant's side.

She cringed as the harshness of his body connected with hers. His free arm hooked painfully around her waist, holding her tight. "Those kisses should be mine, you know."

"Never." Her hand itched to reach up and slap the cocky expression off his face. She wiggled her body in hopes of freeing herself, but Grant just pulled her closer.

"You are mine, Paxton. It was me you promised to marry. Had it not been for that fool over there, we would have been husband and wife by now, and none of this would be happening."

She opened her mouth to tell him what she thought of being a wife to a man like him, but her words halted as his mouth crushed painfully against hers. Bile rose in her throat, and she struggled to break free. His kiss disgusted her as hard, cold lips pressed angrily against hers.

Freeing an arm, she flattened her hand against his chest, and shoved with all her might. Forcing Grant to step backward to keep his balance, she broke the contact. With the back of her hand, she wiped the feel of his lips from her mouth, hating that they had replaced the soft memories of Hunter's kiss a few seconds before.

Hunter moved closer to where she and Grant stood, gray eyes full of an anger she'd never before witnessed in him. Every muscle in his body was rigid. His face was pulled into tight lines of fury. For a moment, she was afraid he was going to storm Grant, regardless of the gun directed squarely at his heart.

"I've had about enough of you two." Grant's voice rose in anger once he steadied himself. "First, I kill lover boy over there. And then I kill you."

Paxton's eyes widened as Grant's finger tightened on the trigger. She had to do something. She couldn't stand there and watch while he shot and killed the man she loved. Her gaze met Hunter's in a plea for their lives.

Without words, he spoke to her, communicating through the bond existing so strongly between them. She saw it in his eyes, read what he wanted from her—

The moment up at the cabin flashed back. They'd been here before, staring down death.

Knowing this was their last chance. Knowing the next few seconds held their future in its hands, she bit down hard on her lip, gathered every last bit of courage she had.

Everything happened in a blur. Paxton lifted her foot, using the pointed toe of her heels to imbed a swift kick at the front of Grant's shin. He howled in pain, dropping the aim of the gun long enough for Hunter to move in.

"Paxton, run," he ordered as Grant quickly regained his composure and lifted the gun.

Breaking free, she saw him raise the gun again as she scampered away. Her heart stopped as he aimed it at her.

"No." Hunter threw his body at Grant as the sound of a gunshot echoed through the air.

She felt the pain a second before she tumbled to the ground. Her arm broke into hot fire as she fell. She cried out from the force of the pain. Her body hit the hard ground, and her head hit with a crack against something hard protruding through the dirt. The last thing she heard before blackness took over was the sound of her name falling from Hunter's lips.

Chapter Twenty

Hunter had never known such fear. In all his years, he'd never felt so helpless…so utterly useless. Pacing back and forth inside the starched white halls of the hospital, he fought to control the tumbling fall of his emotions. He knew it was useless even as he tried.

His hands clenched into fists at his sides as the image of a pale, bleeding Paxton formed in his mind. He'd been so afraid on that mountainside. Afraid of the lifeless pile of her body sprawled on the dirty ground. It wasn't until he placed two fingers to her neck and felt the weak beat of her pulse that he'd released the breath he'd held since witnessing her fall.

He could have literally killed Grant for what he did. Probably would have if his concern for Paxton hadn't overridden the anger surging through. He'd made him hurt though as anger rushed through every punch he delivered.

As soon as Paxton delivered her lethal kick, he'd moved with fierce abandon. But he would forever curse himself for not getting to Grant in time to stop the final shot knocking her off her feet, leaving her life hanging in the balance. He'd left a beaten, limp body sprawled across the ground after he was done with Grant, making sure he wasn't going anywhere for a very long time.

The quiet ring of the elevator pulled him from his thoughts. Shoving his hands into the front pockets of his jeans, he rolled on the heels of his shoes, and studied the man emerging from the sliding doors.

It took less than a second to recognize him. Theodore Walsh walked with a debonair air all his own. He held himself in a way leaving no doubt to the wealth and prestige backing up his family name. Though his hair had silvered, and his stomach had grown wider with the years, he looked like the man Hunter remembered from so long ago.

And, just as they had years ago, his instincts flared, prepared to defend. Squaring his shoulders, every muscle tensed in preparation for a fight as he watched Paxton's father approach.

Worry lines creased his face. As he drew closer, there was no missing his blood-shot eyes or the fear taking over, making him look every bit of his age.

"How is she?" He looked at Hunter, and then past him to the empty waiting room, where a television droned on in the background.

His concern broke through Hunter's defensive wall. As much as he hated to admit it, he found himself feeling sorry for the older man.

Pulling his hands out of his pockets, he eased back the anger as he saw a father rather than an enemy. "I don't know. She's still in surgery. I haven't heard a thing since they brought her in."

Theodore covered his face with his hands, a heart wrenching sob escaping. "I can't believe this happened. And it's my fault. I was the one who helped Grant find her."

Hunter didn't fight the old memories slipping off his shoulders. Though he'd once sworn he'd hold his resentment forever, he found it better to let go. He might not agree with the actions of Paxton's father or the way he controlled her life. But he could see with refined clarity, Theodore tried to do right by his daughter. Though he might have been wrong in more ways than one, he'd believed what he was doing was out of love.

It was as much as a surprise to him as it was to Theodore when he placed a reassuring hand on his shoulder. "Grant had a lot of people fooled. You can't blame yourself."

He sank against the white wall behind him. "If anything happens to her I'll never forgive myself. I should have listened when she begged me not to tell Grant where she was. Should have trusted that she knew what she was talking about, instead of, once again, deciding I knew what was best for her."

"Guilt isn't going to help pull her through. We've all made mistakes we can't change." Hunter saw Grant's gun rising again, and Paxton's body falling to the hard ground. "Now isn't the time to dwell on what we can't change."

Long, uncomfortable minutes passed as Theodore stared at him. He said nothing, showing no signs of hearing anything he'd said. The silence lingered until, finally, he drew a deep breath. "I owe you a thank you for saving my daughter's life."

Uncomfortable with such words coming from the man he'd once considered one of his worst enemies, Hunter tried brushing off his gratitude with a quick wave of his hand.

"No. Let me have my say." He wasn't going to be put off. "No matter what happens to Paxton, we both know she is alive because of you. For that I owe you my life."

He looked past Hunter as if needing to find the words and the strength to continue. "Years ago, I never gave you a chance. I never tried to see in you what my daughter did. I was unfair, and I want to apologize for the harm I caused."

"The past is the past." Hunter shrugged, not sure how to take his words. This was not a time in his life he ever thought would come. Every encounter he envisioned with Paxton's father ended with fists drawn, not with an apology of past wrongs.

"Yes, I suppose it is." Theodore looked so beaten. So drained. A complete opposite to the man he was before. "I just hope both you and Paxton can find it in your hearts to forgive me someday. I hope you both know that your futures are your own, no matter what you make of them."

Hunter knew exactly what he wanted to make of his future with Paxton. He knew in that instant back up on the mountain when he thought, for one horrifying moment, she was dead. He couldn't live without her, regardless of how many times he'd tried to tell himself otherwise.

All these years, he'd only been fooling himself into believing he was over her and didn't need her in his life. She was as vital a part of him as his beating heart. For ten years, he'd walked around empty because of her absence. Only in the past couple weeks had his life become full again.

No. He didn't intend to let Paxton go a second time. He would fight to the ends of the Earth and back to keep her with him. As soon as she came out of this—and he had to believe she would—he intended to lay his feelings out and hope she still felt the same.

"Agent Reese."

He turned, finding a man in green scrubs approaching from the other end of the hall, his hair in disarray. His face showed the stress of a man who had put in many hard hours with little to no rest.

"I'm Dr. Harkins." He offered a hand. "I was Paxton's attending physician during her surgery."

Theodore rushed forward. Rather than elbowing his way past Hunter, as he most surely would have done just a day ago, he stopped side by side with him. "How is my daughter, Doctor? Is she going to be all right?"

"The bullet entered through her shoulder and exited beneath her shoulder blade." Though he kept a professional distance, there was kindness in the doctor's words. "Through its path, it tore some tissues and nicked a couple arteries that needed to be repaired. It doesn't appear to have done any serious damage. Other than the severe concussion she suffered when she hit her head, her injuries are not as serious as we first believed."

The relief was so great, Hunter nearly stumbled under its force. She was going to be okay. A weight as heavy as a ton of bricks lifted from his shoulders.

"Can we see her?" Theodore wrapped an anxious hand around the doctor's arm.

"In time. She's in recovery now, resting. She hasn't regained consciousness. And I want to keep a close eye on her to make sure the blow to her head didn't cause more serious problems than we originally thought."

"In about an hour we'll move her to a private room." He glanced at his watch, nodded as if satisfied with his words. "At that point, we'll allow you in to see her."

Though Hunter ached to see Paxton—see for himself she was okay—he accepted what was offered. He'd wait, just as he knew Theodore would wait, for however long it took to see for themselves that she'd survived the horror.

****

She was falling, unable to stop her downward tumble. The darkness around her was thick, swallowing her away in its depths. Paxton struggled to rise, free herself from its clutches, but each time she tried scrambling away, she lost her grip to tumble all over again.

Frantically she searched for something firm to grasp onto. Something stable to help her escape the unknown. Her fear grew as she continued to fall, until a familiar voice drifted from somewhere far away. She fought the dark, hearing her name called over and over again.

Using it as her lifeline, she clutched desperately to the familiar voice, allowing it to pull her from the darkness. Slowly, she became more aware of a dim light shining up ahead and knew she'd reach her destination if she could just hold on long enough.

The call of her name grew louder, stronger. She gained strength from the sound of the voice. The light ahead grew brighter until the darkness was left behind. It warmed her the instant she stepped into its welcoming arms. For a moment she no longer had an urge to move. She was perfectly content to enjoy the comfort offered.

But the sound of her name beckoned again and she continued on.

"I know you can hear me. Open your eyes for me, princess."

She knew the voice. Knew it like she knew the beat of her own heart.

Hunter.

His name whispered on her lips.

"I'm right here, Paxton."

A gentle squeeze covered her hand. Her eyelids felt as if they weighed a ton. With sheer force of will, she forced them open. Blinding light greeted her. For several minutes, she couldn't see as her eyes struggled to adjust to the sudden intrusion.

"There you are." Hunter's handsome face greeted her as her vision returned. A smile full of tender relief stretched his lips while his gray eyes drew her in, chasing away the lingering chill.

He collected her small hand into his to bring it to his lips and trail gentle kisses across her knuckles. His fingers trembled while he held on to her as if he never wanted to let go. She tightened her fingers around his, offering a small smile to his worried gaze.

His eyes held her captive, peering straight through to her heart. In the intensity of his gaze, unable, and unwilling, to look away, she began to remember.

The images rushed at her, recreating a night she knew was better left forgotten. The dark. The long hike up the mountain. She could feel Hunter's kiss on her lips seconds before Grant had torn her away. The fear running wild through her bones when she thought Grant was going to kill Hunter right before her eyes.

She shivered. A small cry escaped as she saw herself running, Hunter charging after Grant. Then she remembered the pain. The searing streak of fire burning through her right arm before everything went black.

She didn't know what had happened after that. With a deep urgency, her eyes traveled over Hunter. "Are you okay?" The fear she'd felt in that moment before slipping away returned with full force. "I thought…I thought he might have killed you."

"I'm okay." He brushed the hair from her forehead. "It's not me you should be worrying about. You're the one who gave us a fright."

She heard a choked sob from the other side of the bed. Startled, her eyes flew across the small, sterile room.

Sitting in a chair, hidden by the shadows, her father looked like a beaten man. Gone was the power and authority he carried everywhere. Though he tried smiling as her gaze landed on him, he failed, offering nothing more than a pained stretch to his lips.

"Dad." Her voice held a mixture of concern and uncertainty. She held her hand out, wondered why he refused to approach. She looked at Hunter. Was he the reason? Had old pains driven an even deeper wedge between them?

Tugging his chair behind him, her father moved closer. Still keeping distance between them, he extended his long arm and took her hand into his. He squeezed her fingers between his and gazed at her through eyes moist from unshed tears. Sadness etched the lines of his face and left a dark cloud looming over him.

"He's having a hard time," Hunter whispered so he wouldn't be overheard. "He feels responsible for what happened."

She looked at Hunter with wide eyes, unable to

hide the shock kicking to life. He didn't curse her father or throw around his own accusations for her father's part in all that had happened. There was a gentleness to his tone. A compassion she never thought she'd hear from him.

Turning back to her father, she tugged, pulling him closer. She wanted to know what had happened between her father and Hunter, but those questions could wait. First, she had to wipe away the mournful expression stretched across his face.

Pushing up from his chair, he moved closer to stand at the side of her bed. He reached out and pushed the hair from her eyes as he'd done many times when she was a small girl. On some level, she was aware of Hunter quietly sliding back, giving them privacy.

The warmth of his hand slipped from hers. She wanted to protest, demand he stay by her side. But she understood what he was trying to do and didn't stop him as he moved away.

"You're all right." Relief flooded her father's every word. He looked at her as if it had been years, rather than weeks since he last saw her.

She nodded, offering a smile in hopes of easing some of the tension rolling off him. "But you don't look so good."

"I suppose I don't. It's not an easy thing, worrying about your child. I think this has been the longest day of my life. If something had happened to you, I never would have forgiven myself."

"I'm okay." She laid a hand against his rough cheek. "You don't need to beat yourself up."

"I helped lead Grant to you. I didn't listen when you asked me not to tell him where you were. That mistake could have cost you your life. I've been so busy trying to run your life I've forgotten you're all grown up and can make decisions just fine on your own."

Her eyes widened in surprise. This was her father talking? It didn't seem possible. To hear him admit she was capable of running her own life was an experience she never believed she'd have. She never imagined he'd someday cut the strings that kept him treating her as a little girl instead of the adult she'd become.

"I still need my father from time to time." She smiled, hoping to erase some of the hurt chasing over his tight expression. "You may not need to make the decisions for me any longer, but you can still be a part of them."

"As long as I keep my opinion out of it, right?" He offered his first genuine smile, easing some of her worry.

"Well…maybe not always." It was going to take some time getting used to a new relationship with her father. She might not have liked his ways on many occasions, but she loved him and had come to accept him as the forceful, overprotective father he was. A change in their relationship was going to affect both of them, charting new territory neither one knew how to travel down.

Bending down, he brushed a fatherly kiss across her forehead. "I love you. You know that, don't you?"

A knot formed in her throat and she nodded. A single tear escaped, trailing slowly down her cheek. Such words were not easily spoken by a man like her father. To hear them, hear the emotion behind them, spoke volumes of what was being shared between them.

"I love you too." She didn't try to stop the single tear slipping from the corner of her eye.

With the pad of his finger, her father gently wiped it away. "I think, when you're feeling better, the two of us need to sit down, and have a long talk, just between father and daughter."

She nodded, actually looking forward to it. Though she knew better than to believe everything would be perfect between them. She felt a certain excitement knowing maybe—just maybe—they'd turned an important corner in their relationship and might actually find something so much better than what they'd had.

"For now, though—" Her father curled his fingers softly against her cheek. "There is a young man over there who I've taken enough time away from. I'm going to go, give you some privacy. But I'll be back to check on you."

Leaving another kiss on the top of her brow, he turned away from the bed. On his way out the door, he paused where Hunter had slipped back into the shadows.

Paxton watched her father offer a hand and Hunter take it without hesitation. A silent communication passed between them before her father waved at her once more then disappeared out the door, closing it tightly behind him.

Trying to sit up as Hunter returned, she found the pain shooting through her arm and shoulder was too great to ignore. With a muffled cry, she sank back down onto the bed. Her head spinning.

He was at her side in a second, resting a hand against her arm. "Don't you dare try to move." He fluffed the pillow behind her head and eased her back.

"You've been unconscious for almost twenty-four hours and in surgery for four hours. Your body needs time to rest."

"I was shot, wasn't I?" She sucked in a deep breath as the pain eased.

He nodded. "Through the shoulder. Thankfully, the bullet missed major organs. It was the knock on the head when you fell that caused some of the worst damage."

Reaching up, she found the egg-sized bump on the side of her left temple. "How did I get here?" She waved her hand around the room.

Satisfied she wouldn't try sitting up again, Hunter reclaimed the chair at the edge of her bed and gathered her hand into his. "Grant had his phone with him. The service was terrible but it was enough to get a message through. It was awhile before the Bureau located us stuffed so deep in the mountains. But once they got there, they wasted no time in getting you to the hospital."

"And Grant?" Paxton held her breath, wanting yet fearing the answer.

"He was examined in the emergency room last night then taken into custody. Tony is singing like a bird, and with kidnapping and attempted murder charges now filed against him, he won't be seeing the light of day again."

Relief washed over her with the force of a flooding river. Danger no longer hovered above her head, allowing her to return to the freedom she'd once known. Her life could go back to normal. Back to the way it was before Grant was involved.

Sorrow choked her with the last thought. Stealing a

glance at Hunter, her relief disappeared. Grant was gone. Would Hunter be as well? There was no reason for him to stay any longer. The danger was over. She didn't need him to protect her. It was time for him to say goodbye.

Goodbye.

The thought tore at her heart. They never had a chance to discuss what was going to happen between them. She knew what she wanted. What did Hunter want? Could he trust her again? Believe in her enough to know she would never let him go as she had foolishly done before.

"Paxton." Her name fell softly from his lips.

She glanced his way, knowing her every emotion showed on her face. She didn't think she could handle the pain if he told her he didn't want her in his life. Tears choked the back of her throat as she thought of losing him again.

With his finger, he brushed away the tear that escaped. "You're all right now."

He mistook the reason for her tears.

"You'll never have to fear Grant again."

She shook her head as another tear escaped. She wanted to tell him she wasn't crying over Grant, could care less about him, but she couldn't get the words to form.

Seeing more tears, he collected her in his arms, careful not to add any more pain to her injuries. "He won't hurt you ever again. I promise."

"It's not Grant." Her voice shook with the pain she tried shoving away. Reaching up, she brushed at the tears falling down her cheeks. With a deep breath, she collected herself and calmed the frantic beat of her heart. "I'm not afraid of him. I don't care to ever think about him again."

"Then why the tears?" He tightened his arm around her, pulling her close enough to hear the steady beat of his heart and the long, powerful draw of each breath he took.

She couldn't put into words what she felt, too afraid of answers that might come.

Hunter pulled back and gave her a long, probing look. It wouldn't be hard for him to see the truth. There was no sense in trying to hide the fact she was afraid of losing him again. She loved him. If she had to remind him of that over and over again she would.

He smiled at her, a touch of amusement in the lift of his lips. "I recall something about the two of us needing to talk when the mess with Grant was over with."

Swallowing over the nervous lump in her throat, she nodded.

"Well…I don't think that's necessary any longer. Everything that could have been said, has been said. I don't believe there is anything more to say."

Her heart fell. A pain tore through her that was worse than any of the pain from her physical injuries. He was going to say goodbye. She couldn't blame him. She'd done the exact same thing ten years ago.

She was going to lose Hunter all over again. After a strange twist of fate brought them back together, they were again going their separate ways. The hurt pounding against her chest was so great, she wasn't sure how she was going to make it through his farewell.

"There's just one thing left unsaid between us," he carried on as if he noticed none of the tension vibrating through her or the fear clutching at her. Didn't he notice her hands closing in a desperate grip around his? See the plea in her eyes?

She did her best to block out his next words. It was bad enough to have him say goodbye. To hear him actually say the words was more than she could handle.

"...marry me?"

She blinked in surprise. There was something in what he was saying she must have heard wrong. In her efforts to drown him out, she'd only picked up the tail end of his words and was sure she had made a mistake in what she heard.

"Paxton." He moved in closer, cupping one cheek with his hand. "Did you hear what I asked you?"

"I'm not sure." Maybe it was the knock to her head leaving her confused. Or the uncontrolled swirl of emotions racing through. Whatever it was, it chased away her grasp on clear thought.

"I asked you to marry me. I'm asking you to spend the rest of your life with me and build a family with me." He tightened his hold on her hand, gazing at her with eyes baring his soul. "I love you. I've always loved you. I can't imagine spending another day without you at my side."

Tears filled her eyes. But this time they were tears of joy—the best kind to have.

He wanted to marry her. He wanted to spend the rest of his life with her.

Images of sunny days started with him at her side, long nights making love, rushed through her mind. He'd make a wonderful husband. And she'd make him the best wife she could.

"Do I get an answer?" He raised his eyebrows

when there was still no response.

"Yes. Oh yes." Ignoring the pain shooting through her arm, she threw herself around him. "Marrying you will be a dream come true."

"Thank goodness." Hunter gave an exaggerated sigh of relief. "I was hoping I wouldn't have to go through with plan B."

"Plan B?" She looked at him with questioning eyes as he tightened his hold around her.

He nodded. "It consisted of me camping out on your doorstep day and night until you finally agreed to marry me. I figured sooner or later, you'd have to agree."

"No Plan B." She shook her head. "But I do have one request before marrying you."

There was amusement, not worry, in his eyes as he trailed light kisses up and down her cheeks. "What would that be?"

Trying to keep a clear head through the fog of his sweet kisses, she forced her mind to function long enough to finish the conversation. "This time at the church, for my wedding day, I'd like to get around on my own two feet. As much as I love being swept up in your arms and pray it happens often, the whole over-the-shoulder carry really kind of ruined the look of my wedding gown."

"You have my promise," he vowed, dropping a soft kiss on her lips.

"I tell you what," he pulled away, letting her see the mischievous glint in his gray eyes. "I'll save my over-the-shoulder carry for after the wedding when I take you straight to bed."

"Promise?" Her body kicked to life with images of

just what would happen when Hunter got her into that bed of his.

"I promise."

A word about the author…

Cassandra Bella is an author of romance suspense novels. Discover more about her and her books at cassandrabella.net